D0676571

Also by Jean Ure

Hunky Dory
Gone Missing
Over the Moon
Boys Beware
Sugar and Spice
Is Anybody There?
Secret Meeting
Passion Flower
Shrinking Violet
Boys on the Brain
Skinny Melon and Me
Becky Bananas, This is Your Life!
Fruit and Nutcase
The Secret Life of Sally Tomato*
Family Fan Club

Special three-in-one editions

The Tutti-Frutti Collection
The Flower Power Collection
The Friends Forever Collection

and for younger readers

Dazzling Danny
Daisy May
Monster in the Mirror

**Also available on tape, read by John Pickard*

Jean Ure

HarperCollins *Children's Books*

For Eloise Slaughter

First published in Great Britain by HarperCollins *Children's Books* in 2008
HarperCollins *Children's Books* is a division of HarperCollins*Publishers* Ltd,
77-85 Fulham Palace Road, Hammersmith, London W6 8JB

The HarperCollins *Children's Books* website address is
www.harpercollinschildrensbooks.co.uk

2

Text © Jean Ure 2008
Illustrations © HarperCollins*Publishers* 2008

The author and illustrator assert the moral right to be
identified as the author and illustrator of this work.

ISBN-13: 978-0-00-722461-6
ISBN-10: 0-00-722461-3

Printed and bound in England by
Clays Ltd, St Ives plc

Conditions of Sale
This book is sold subject to the condition that it shall not,
by way of trade or otherwise, be lent, re-sold, hired out or otherwise
circulated without the publisher's prior consent in any form, binding or
cover other than that in which it is published and without a similar condition
including this condition being imposed on the subsequent purchaser.

CHAPTER ONE

The day Marigold Johnson called me a fat freak was the day I started bunking off school.

That is a fact. It is absolutely one hundred per cent true. But is it a good way to begin? I thought that it was, but now I am not so sure. I mean, in one sense it was what *set things in motion*, as they say, cos if it hadn't been for me bunking off school – well! Certain things would never have happened. Meeting Mrs P, for one. On the other hand, lots of really significant stuff had gone on in my life before Marigold went and called me a freak. So now I'm feeling a bit confused and don't quite know *how* to begin.

Maybe I should start by explaining about Marigold, and why it was she had it in for me. She still does have it in for me. She's had it in for me ever since Year 7, and we're in Year 9 now. That is what I call bearing a grudge. *With a vengeance.* In other words, she got the hump and has never got over it. It squats there on her shoulder like a big black toad and makes her really mean.

What it was, it was in drama one day when Mrs Hendricks told us to "Partner off, boy and girl." Quite honestly I didn't think anyone would be falling over themselves to partner me. Not that I have an inferiority complex, or anything; Nan always taught me that it's important to value yourself. But there's no point hiding your head in the sand. I'm not the sort of girl that boys fight over, and that is just something I have to live with. Me and a few million others. We can't all look like Marigold Johnson, i.e. stick thin with big pouty lips full of Botox, or whatever it is they put into lips to make them puff up. If she hasn't had Botox (or whatever it is) then she's suffering from some kind of birth defect. One which boys, it has to be said, do seem to be attracted to. I guess big pouty lips are good for slurpy kissing.

Anyway. As soon as Mrs Hendricks said "Partner off", everyone started shuffling about trying to catch the attention of someone they fancied, with me doing my best to fade into the background, which is not easy when you're my size. Even Nan wouldn't have said I was small. Out of the corner of my eye I could see this boy standing just nearby. Well, it was Josh, actually, only I didn't think of him as Josh back then, cos I didn't really know him all that well. He was just a boy who happened to be in my class, so I thought of him as Joshua. Joshua Daniels.

Out of the corner of my other eye I could see Marigold. She was on the move, heading straight past me, straight for… Josh. I guessed that she was out to nab him. See, this was before she started going out with Lance Stapleton, otherwise known as the Thug. The Thug wasn't going out with anyone at that stage, he was too busy charging about in a gang and beating people up. In fact beating people up is still one of his main hobbies, but now he likes to have a girl to watch him do it. I guess it makes him feel important. He and Marigold are dead right for each other. The perfect couple! She wouldn't have suited Josh *at all.* But I knew she fancied him cos I'd seen her flapping her eyes and doing this weird munching thing with her lips. Any second now…

I could hardly bear to watch. It was like some kind of man-eating spider moving in on its prey. *I'm gonna get you!*

And then, quite suddenly, at the last minute, Josh did this about-turn. "Wanna be partners?" he said.

Who? Who was he talking to? Surely not me?

He was! He was talking to me! *Josh* was talking to *me*.

I didn't jump on him, cos that would have been too demeaning; I think you have to have a *bit* of pride. I said, "Yeah! OK," making like it was no big deal, whereas in fact I was still practically reeling from the shock. I mean, who in their right senses would prefer me to Marigold??? Not doing myself down, or anything, but I'd been so sure they'd end up together. I bet she had, too! Cos girls like her, they're always sure. They are not prey to doubts like the rest of us.

Anyway, she was left with Barnaby Tibbs, who is a sweet boy but seriously uncool. She hated me for that. I mean, *hated.* She couldn't stand the thought of a boy she fancied actually ignoring her and going for a lesser being – especially when the lesser being was me. "Carmen Bell! That great *jelly.*"

From then on, that was her name for me: the Great Jelly. Or more usually just the Jelly.

"Where's the Jelly?" "Trust the Jelly!"

I guess I could have retaliated by calling her Botox Lips, or asking her if she'd been dropped on her head as a baby, seeing as her brain appeared to have some kind of malfunction, but that would have meant bringing myself down to her level. I wouldn't give her the satisfaction.

Indy used to tell me that I ought to hit back. She got really agitated about it. "Why don't you stick up for yourself?"

I could have done. I can give as good as I get any day of the week! Mum's always said I've got a mouth on me. Indy just couldn't understand it. "People like that shouldn't be allowed to get away with things! She's a horrible person. She's a *bully*."

I said that she also had the intellectual capacity of a mushy pea, and it would quite simply be beneath me to engage in any sort of conversational exchange. "Who wants to have a slanging match with a pea?"

It just made me feel better if I ignored her. That

way I could at least pretend to myself that I didn't care. If I'd done what Indy wanted and hurled insults, it would be like admitting she'd got to me. I wasn't going to let her!

But I couldn't stop Indy simmering and seething. One day she just, like, boiled over and laid into Marigold big time. Marigold's eyes practically shot out on stalks. I could see she was really taken aback. I was, too! Indy is so tiny, like a little jumping bean, and she's not at all an aggressive sort of person. If anything, she is quite meek. I thought it was incredibly loyal of her, and that I was lucky to have her as a friend, but at the same time I sort of wished she hadn't done it cos it just made Marigold meaner than ever. She sneered down at Indy from her great beanpole height and said, "Naff off, squit face!" And then she made her eyes go crossed and sucked her bottom lip so that her teeth stuck out, and Ashlee Stott, who's like her personal doormat, gave this mad shriek of laughter and started making her teeth stick out, too.

It was such a disgusting thing to do; Indy is really sensitive about her teeth. I felt so bad for her! I think some of the others did, too, but they weren't going to say anything. Marigold is one of those people, nobody really *likes* her, apart from the creep Ashlee, but everyone wants to stay on the right side of her. I told Indy that in future we would both of us ignore her.

"If she thinks she's getting to you, it'll just make her worse."

My theory was that if we took no notice she'd grow bored and start on someone else. Only she didn't, cos of this great vengeance thing and bearing grudges. She went on calling me Jelly, and after a bit other people started calling me Jelly as well. I don't think most of them did it to be mean; it was just a name that had caught on. Marigold was the one that was mean. Mean as maggots, and dripping poison.

Even Josh had a go at her one day. There was a group of us arrived early for a double period of art. We were sitting around in the studio, waiting for the rest of the class to show up, and Marigold was holding court, the way she did, mouthing off about this game show that had been on TV the night before where some poor girl had been made fun of and reduced to tears by the woman that was hosting it. I'd seen the show and I'd felt really sorry for the girl, but Marigold was, like, *She got what she deserved.*

"Should have had a bag over her head!"

Ashlee sniggered and said, "Should have had a bag over her whole body."

"Yeah, right! Talk about a sack of potatoes. I mean, for God's sake, what did she expect?"

"Probably expected to be treated like a human being," I said.

"It's television, *dummy*. It's a *game* show. Anyone looks that grotesque is asking for it."

I said, "What have looks got to do with it? It's not supposed to be about looks, it's supposed to be about personality."

"Yeah, well..." Marigold gave a little smirk. Really

irritating. "You would say that, wouldn't you?"

That was when Josh entered the fray. I didn't think he'd even been listening. Mostly the boys kept out of it when Marigold was doing her spouting. They probably reckoned it was girl stuff and didn't want to be involved. Can't say I blame them. But Josh was in earshot and I guess he just couldn't resist. Without even looking up, he muttered, "Talk about having sawdust where your brains ought to be."

Marigold spun round like she'd been shot. Indy giggled, and Marigold went bright red. It was such a good moment! But after that she was more vengeful than ever. The idea of a *boy* having a go at her – well, I don't think it had ever happened before. Boys always fancied her like crazy. Now she had it in for Josh as well as me and Indy, but it was me she had it in for most. I didn't care! Her spiteful remarks just went right over my head.

So, that is all about Marigold and how she came to hate me. I think now it's probably time to move on. I'll fast forward to the start of the summer term – last summer term, when we were in Year 8. Always, in July, our school has a Charity Fun Day, when we do things that are supposed to be fun to raise money for good causes. I say *supposed* to be fun cos sometimes they just aren't. Like in Year 7 when we had this massive tug-of-war and I got chosen to be the anchor person for our class. Not one of the boys: *me*. Needless to say, it was Marigold's idea. She said, "Shut up, Jelly! It's for charity." Indy, trying to make me feel better, said that at least it showed we weren't sexist, but it was still quite humiliating.

I wasn't particularly looking forward to this year's event, wondering somewhat glumly what new fun things the committee would be dreaming up, but then when the notice went on the board… yay! I couldn't believe it! We were going to have a talent contest!!! And not one of the boring sort that teachers normally go for, where people get up and recite endless lines of poetry or play bits of tuneless tinkly stuff on the piano and everyone is, like, *Yawn, how much longer is this going on?* This time it was to be a *pop* contest.

TOP SPOT, for all you aspiring pop stars out there!

Indy saw it first and rushed to find me, squeaking excitedly. "Carm, Carm, come and look!"

My first thought was that it would only be for seniors, but it didn't say that it was.

"It's for everyone," said Indy. "See? Says there... they'll be asking for names..." She peered closer. Indy is quite short-sighted, and won't always wear her glasses. "*...in a week or two.* Says anyone can enter, but you have to be serious. You're serious!"

I was. *I am!* I have wanted to be a pop star ever since I can remember – well, a rock star, actually, as I have this really BIG voice. Nan used to say, "That girl is star crazy!"

I was so excited. I stayed awake all night, wondering

what to sing, wondering what to wear. Indy was excited, too; excited for *me*. She is so loyal! She said we should go into town on Saturday and choose an outfit. She said it was important I should get it settled well in advance. "Cos you know with new clothes you have to wear them for a bit. Just at home! Not outdoors. Don't want to get them dirty, or anything. But you gotta make sure they're comfortable."

She was right! I asked Mum if it would be OK for me to go clothes shopping. Mum said yes, no problem. I knew she would! She's funny like that. When I was desperate, and I mean *desperate*, to have a guitar, she told me that it was "just a phase" I was going through and it would be a sheer waste of money (which meant I had to wait for Christmas, which at that point was ten whole months away). When I begged her for an iPod she screamed at me that she was a single mum. "I'm doing the best I can!" I never did get the iPod. Like with DVDs or CDs she tells me to go and borrow them from the library: "I'm not made of money!" But clothes… clothes are a different matter.

Looking good is very important to Mum; I guess because she works in a beauty parlour. She herself is thin as a pin, the reason being that she picks at her food and smokes like a chimney, which I have tried but found it to be so totally and utterly disgusting that it nearly made me sick. Besides, it smells. Mum smells. Stale cigarette smoke wafts all about her, but she doesn't care just so long as she is *thin*. Having a daughter who is anything but thin is a cross that Mum has to bear. It is very hard on her. I think sometimes she despairs, though she does her best to be optimistic. She lives in hope that the next new skirt/top/pair of trousers I buy will miraculously transform me from a jelly to a stick insect.

She said that she could let me have fifty pounds. "Not a penny more! What sort of thing were you thinking of getting?"

I said I didn't know. I was going to look round and see what took my fancy.

"Maybe I ought to come with you."

Oh God, I didn't want Mum going with me! It makes me so embarrassed. Knowing that every single garment she picks out will look far better on her than it does on me. I told her that Indy was coming and we were going to choose together.

Mum said, "Indy? That funny little thing? She has no more sense of fashion than you do!"

This, unfortunately, is perfectly true. Indy and I are not very cool when it comes to clothes.

"OK," I said. "I'll ask Josh!"

"That's more like it," said Mum.

She knows that Josh can be relied upon. He's going to go to art college when he leaves school and train to be a fashion designer. He's promised me that when we are both famous he will design all my clothes for me, even if I am still a jelly. (Josh didn't say that last bit; that was me.)

Saturday morning we met at the bus stop and took the bus into town, where Indy was waiting for us in the

Arcade, outside Top Shop. Josh said, "We'll start in here and work our way round. You'll have to be prepared to spend the whole morning, if necessary." He'd automatically taken charge, but that was all right; me and Indy didn't mind. We followed meekly in his wake, with me doing my best not to let my eyes stray towards racks of gorgeous but totally unsuitable gear. Unsuitable for me, that is. Josh had said sternly that I mustn't be a slave to fashion, and I knew what he meant. It wasn't the least bit of use me hankering after miniskirts or crop tops, cos he wouldn't let me have them.

"You have to create your own style! Be original."

Indy, greatly daring, said, "What about one of those nice long floaty skirts?"

Josh said, "For a rock chick?"

Indy giggled. "Is that what she is?"

"Not in a long skirt," said Josh.

I was glad about that cos although it would hide my legs I'd probably only go and trip over it. I can be a bit clumsy when I get nervous.

"*These.*" Josh suddenly lunged at a nearby rack and thrust something at me.

"Combats," said Indy. "That's cool!"

Somewhat nervously – I am always nervous when it comes to clothes – I said, "D'you really think so?"

"Are you daring to question me?" said Josh.

"No!" I backed down, hastily.

"So take them! Try them."

"What about a top?" said Indy.

"I'm coming to that," said Josh. "Don't rush me!"

Indy and I exchanged glances. Talk about a prima donna! Humbly, we trailed round after him.

"Here! Try this." He picked up a T-shirt and handed it to me.

"Ooh, designer!" said Indy.

"It's just a T-shirt," said Josh.

But it wasn't! I looked at the price tag and nearly died. *All that,* for a T-shirt? Josh said, "Quality does not come cheap." Then he gave me a little push in the direction of the changing room and said, "Well, go on, go and try them on!"

"And then come out and show us," said Indy.

I never enjoy trying on clothes. Whatever I buy, it's always the same: I look in the mirror and there's this great galumphing hippopotamus staring back at me. I couldn't see that combats and a T-shirt, no matter if the T-shirt did cost the earth, were likely to work any miracles. But oh, they did! The T-shirt didn't just flump about in big billowing folds, the same as T-shirts usually do. It actually fitted. *Properly.* It was red, with a skull and crossbones motif on the front. I loved it! It almost made me look thin. Well, thinn*ish.*

The combats, which were half the price of the T-shirt, were olive green, and wonder of wonders, I managed to get into them without any straining or heaving or sucking in of my tummy. I went prancing out of the changing room with this big, triumphant grin on my face.

Indy took one look and squealed, "Rock chick!"

"See?" Josh gave a little bow. "Apology graciously accepted."

"So what's she going to wear with it?" said Indy.

I said, "Yes! What am I going to wear with it?" The T-shirt by itself had eaten up a large chunk of Mum's money. Josh said not to panic. "You don't really need anything else."

"What about shoes?" said Indy.

"Trainers," said Josh.

"What about jewellery?"

Josh said so long as it wasn't clunky.

"Let's go and look!" Indy went dancing off up the store, to where they had a stand full of beads and bangles. "Look, look, what about this?" She came dancing back, dangling a long silver chain with a pendant. "This would go! Wouldn't it?"

She was ever so happy when Josh agreed. It made her a bit bold. Eagerly she suggested that maybe I could buy some "dangly earrings" and "sparkly bits to put in my hair". Josh said, "Knock it off, she's a rock chick, not a Christmas tree!" Indy's face fell. "Maybe something for her hair," said Josh.

"And nail varnish?" begged Indy. "She could have nail varnish!"

Josh said he would allow me to have nail varnish, and he even let Indy pick the colour: deep, dark purple.

"Don't ask me what *I'd* like," I said.

"Got no intention," said Josh. "*I'm* your fashion guru."

"And I'm his assistant," giggled Indy. It was really going to her head! But I didn't mind; I know I have no clothes sense. They didn't even let me choose the sparkly bits for my hair. Personally I rather fancied a pair of glittery butterflies, but Indy sucked in her breath and Josh, very sternly, said, "Carm, put them back."

"But they're pretty!"

"They're tacky."

"Tacky, tacky, tacky!" sang Indy. Like she knows any better than I do. "Look, stars! How about stars?"

Josh said yes, stars would do fine.

Indy beamed. "Stars for a star! Cos that's what she's going to be."

"I dunno." I shook my head. "It's all very well getting stuff to wear, but what am I gonna sing?"

"We'll work on it," said Josh. "Maybe write something special."

Yesss! I felt like flying at him and hugging him, only he'd probably just have got embarrassed. But I was really excited by the idea. A song written specially for the occasion! It might even gain me some extra points.

As soon as I got home, Mum demanded to know what I'd bought. "Put it on, so I can see!"

I was a bit wary, cos Mum is just, like, *so* critical, but I could tell at once that she approved.

"Wonderful," she said, "to have a boyfriend who can choose clothes for you!"

I have told Mum so many times that Josh is *not my boyfriend*. He is just a friend who happens to be a boy. Mum doesn't believe that is possible. She once said so in front of Nan. She said, "You can't have a *boy* as a *friend*. Not just an ordinary *friend*." Then she laughed and said, "Well, I never could."

Nan, quick as a flash, said, "No, and look what happened to you!" Nan could be quite sharp, and she always, *always* defended me. I do miss her loads. She used to tell Mum to leave me alone, especially when Mum nagged at me about my weight, or said if Josh wasn't my boyfriend then wasn't it about time I got one?

I've had boyfriends! Two, in fact. One was Sam Wyman that lives in our block, and the other was Judd Priestley at juniors. They were both unimaginably *boring*. You couldn't ever talk to them like I can with Josh. When I said this to Mum she raised both eyebrows and said, "Who wants a boyfriend for *talking* to?"

I said, "I do!" To which Mum retorted that I would "sing a different tune one of these days". Well, pardon me, but I don't think so!

Next weekend, I got together with Josh and we

wrote a song for me to sing in the talent contest. We've been writing songs for ever. We started back in Year 7, and we're still doing it. We work really well together. Sometimes we argue, but we never fall out. We tend to bounce ideas off each other, like Josh will say, "How about this?" and I'll say, "Or maybe this?" and that will set us off and get us all inspired in a way that I don't think would happen if we were doing it separately. We work out the music together, too. I play the guitar – well, just chords mainly, on account of being self-taught – but Josh is like a demon on the keyboard and the drums. He knows about music because his mum and dad are musicians. His dad is a violinist and plays in an orchestra, his mum teaches at a local school. Josh always claims not to be musical – he says I am far more musical than he is – but he knows things that I don't, so I'll, like, sing a phrase and Josh will pick it up and run with it. Between us, we're an ace team!

This is the song that we wrote:

Star crazy me
Floatin' free-ee-ee
Into the ether of
Eternity

Now do you see me
Ridin' high
Ridin' high
Streamers of song
'Cross the sky-y-y

Nobody nothing
Ain't gonna stop
This crazy crazy crazy gal
This crazy gal
Will reach the top
Oh yeah
Oh yeah

Just watch me, babe
I'm floatin' free
I'm flyin' high-igh-igh

Gonna get there
Gonna be
Up there for all eternity
Oh yeah
Oh yeah

Star crazy me
I'm floatin' free

I said to Josh that we should both enter the contest, me as vocalist, him on the keyboard, but he wouldn't. He said, "Don't bully me! You're always bullying me."

I said, "Me bully *you*? That's a joke!"

If either of us gets to be bullied, I'd say that it was me. Josh can be really bossy at times! Like he'll tell me, for instance, that "You can't possibly wear that top with that skirt, it makes you look like a parcel," and I will immediately rush back indoors and change, cos I know that he knows about such things. I mean, I will just go and *do* it. No argument! Josh, on the other hand, tends to go all quiet and dig his heels in.

I said, "I'm just trying to give you your share of the limelight. Credit where credit's due." As Nan used to say.

Josh said he didn't want credit. "And I don't want limelight! I'm not like you."

"You're just scared!" I said.

"I'm modest," said Josh.

I teased him about that. I said, "Aah, sweet! He's all shy and retiring!" And I chucked him under the chin, really yucky, just to get him going, and he said "Gerroff!" and we had a bit of a tussle, all over the bed and round his bedroom, until his mum yelled at us up the stairs.

"What are you doing up there? You'll bring the ceiling down!"

"You are just *so* childish," said Josh.

"And you are just *so* stubborn!" I said.

He still wouldn't budge. He said that I was the performer, not him, and I think that is probably right. Josh is more of a behind-the-scenes person, which wouldn't do at all for me. I just love the buzz of being out there, in the spotlight, in front of an audience. Actually, to be honest, I hadn't ever really performed in front of an audience at that point, except once in Year 6 when we put on a little end-of-term show and I was chosen to sing a Christmas carol. I belted it out at the top of my voice and Mrs Deakin, our teacher, got really upset. She seemed to think I was showing off. She said, "Honestly, Carmen! That was totally inappropriate."

Well, but I did enjoy it! *And* I got a round of applause. So you can imagine I was really looking forward to the talent contest and singing our song. As soon as the notice appeared on the board – **Entrants for Top Spot, sign here** – I rushed to put my name down.

Carmen Bell Year 8 Vocalist

And that was when Marigold Johnson called me a fat freak, and ruined it all.

CHAPTER TWO

This is where it happened: in the locker room at school. Me and Indy were already down there, putting stuff away and sorting out what we needed for afternoon classes. The Year 8 lockers are in two rows, back to back, with a few odd ones tucked away in a corner, out of sight. Me and Indy were in the tucked-away part. In other words, nobody knew that we were there. We weren't eavesdropping! We weren't crouched on the ground with our ears pinned back. But when Marigold came bursting in with her usual crowd of gawkers and her mouth clattering on at about a hundred miles per hour, we couldn't help hearing.

What she was clattering on about was the Top Spot contest. How her sister, Mary-Louise, that was in Year 10, was almost certain to win because *she* had professional experience. *She* had appeared in a commercial. *She* had made a demo disc.

"It really isn't fair on all the others, but what can you do? My sister can't be stopped from putting her name down just because she's had experience."

Then we heard Ashlee's voice piping up: "Know who else has put her name down? The Jelly!"

"The *Jelly*? You gotta be joking!"

OK, so that was when I should probably have emerged from my corner and shown myself, before Marigold could go on and say something nasty. But I didn't, and I bet most people wouldn't have, either. In that sort of situation, you just freeze to the spot and can't move. The very *last* thing you want is for anyone to know that you're there. It's too humiliating.

I heard Ashlee's voice again: "I'm not joking! I just saw her name on the list."

And then Marigold, with her loud braying laugh: "That fat freak? Just cos her stupid old nan reckoned she was gonna be the next Judy Garland. Pur-lease!"

I could sense Indy next to me, holding her breath. Her hand reached out and dabbed at my arm, but I couldn't bring myself to look at her. I just felt so ashamed.

Someone said, "I think she fancies herself as some kind of rock chick."

"*Rock* chick? Excuse me while I die laughing!"

Ashlee said, "Rock *elephant*, more like."

"Rock *jelly*, more like!"

"What d'you think she'll sing?"

"I know what she'll sing, I know what she'll sing!

Like this, look… *sh-shake, w-wobble and ROLL!*"

Delighted shrieks of laughter, as from the sound of things Marigold hurled herself to and fro against the lockers.

"*Sh-shake, w-w-w-WOBBLE and—*"

"Drop dead, pea brain!"

I don't know what came over me, I really don't. But all of a sudden it was like this tidal wave of absolute fury crashed into me, and I leaped out from behind my locker and *yelled:*

"STUPID PEA-BRAINED BLUBBER-LIPPED MORON!"

There was a kind of shocked silence. Marigold was the one that dished it out, not the one that had it dished up. She stared at me like she couldn't believe what she'd heard. Then she took up a stance, her hands on her hips.

"*What* did you say?"

"I said" – I put my face up close to hers – "you're a **STUPID, PEA-BRAINED, BLUBBER-LIPPED**

MORON! And in case you don't know what that means, which you probably don't, it means you're so dumb you're practically a walking vegetable!"

Somebody tittered, rather nervously. Ashlee gave a little horrified squeal, and clapped a hand to her mouth.

"Why don't you go and plant yourself?" I said. "Do us all a favour. Take root!"

With that, I flung open the door and prepared to stalk out. But Marigold had the last word. As I made my grand exit she bawled after me, "Get lost, you pathetic fag hag!"

That was when I bunked off school.

I didn't do it on purpose. I mean, I didn't actually say to myself, "I am going to bunk off school and never come back." It was just something that happened. I got as far as the main corridor and was about to turn up the stairs when this feeling of absolute despair came flooding over me. I couldn't take it any more! I had to get out. *Now.*

I muttered at Indy that I'd left one of my books behind – "You go on, I'll see you up there" – then I turned and fled. Back the way we'd come, through the double doors, across the parking lot and OUT.

The only other time I'd done anything like it was in Year 4, when I got told off for something that wasn't my fault, and when I protested that "It wasn't me!" the teacher wouldn't believe me, and I was so incensed that I slipped out of the gates when no one was looking and ran all the way home to pour out my tale of woe to Nan. Nan agreed with me that it wasn't fair. She said, "Sometimes, chickabiddy, life is like that. You have to be strong, and take the rough with the smooth."

Just knowing that Nan was on my side had made me feel better. But Nan wasn't there any more; she'd never call me chickabiddy ever again, or pass on her words of wisdom. I was on my own, now, cos Mum would never take my side. When I'd told *her* about the teacher being so mean, all she'd said was that she didn't blame her. "You've caused enough problems in your time."

No point trying to cry on Mum's shoulder. I wouldn't, anyway; it was something too shameful ever to tell anyone. But I would have told Nan! She was the one who had faith in me, the one who made me believe in myself. Just that morning, rummaging about for a clean T-shirt, I'd come across the last birthday card that Nan had ever sent me. She'd chosen it so carefully! On the front it had a picture of a groovy guy with a guitar, belting out *Happy Birthday*. Inside, in her shaky handwriting, Nan had written, *To my own little star, who one of these days is going to shine so brightly!*

I'd hidden it away in my secret place, beneath the lining paper at the bottom of a drawer. I'd never shown it to Mum. It was something precious, and I couldn't bear the thought that she might laugh. I think, actually, that was what made me finally turn on Marigold, the fact that she'd dared to bring my nan into it. *Her stupid old nan.* I wished I'd never, ever told anyone about Nan!

But it was back in Year 6, when I'd sung the Christmas carol too loud and upset Mrs Deakin. Defiantly I'd told her that "My nan says I'm going to be a second Judy Garland!" Sometimes when you're only ten you say things you later wish with all your heart that you hadn't.

If I hadn't been chosen to sing the carol – *if* I hadn't sung the carol too loud – *if* I hadn't boasted about Nan... if none of those things had happened then maybe I wouldn't have yelled at Marigold and bunked off school. But I had, and all I could think was that it was fate. There's nothing you can do about fate.

When I got back to the flats I ran into one of our neighbours, Mrs Henson. She said, "Got the afternoon off, have you?"

I gave her a sickly smile and said, "Gotta headache." I hoped she wouldn't mention anything to Mum but I feared the worst. She is a notorious gasbag.

The minute I was inside the flat, with the door closed against the outside world, I began to feel a bit less fraught. I spent the rest of the afternoon sprawled on the sofa, headphones clamped to my ears with the volume turned up as loud as I could bear, listening to all my favourite tracks played by all my favourite bands. Mostly Urban Legend, cos they are like my Favourite of Favourites. Mum can't stand them – she says they're foul-mouthed and violent. *I* say that life is enough to make you foul-mouthed and violent, what with wars going on all over the place, and toxic waste covering the earth, and the polar ice caps melting. Not to *mention* terrorism. To which Mum just goes, "Don't give me isms! Give me *tunes.*" Mum isn't what I would call musical.

Nan, on the other hand, used to really enjoy listening to rock. I don't think she liked it as much as her beloved show tunes – *Over the Rainbow*, and *Oh What a Beautiful Morning*, and all that – but she did once say she'd like to come to a rock concert with me.

"I could scream and throw me knickers on stage! That's what you do, isn't it? Throw your knickers? I could get into that!"

Mum said, "At your age? You ought to be ashamed!"

But Nan wasn't ashamed of anything, which is why I try so hard not to be. Especially not of my own body. After all, it's the one I was born with and I can't help the way it is. It's not like I gorge on junk food. It's not like I don't get any exercise. *Mum* doesn't; she goes everywhere by car. Not me! I walk to and from the bus stop every day, and more often than not I walk up the stairs as well, all ten flights of them. I only take the lift if I'm feeling really knackered. I hate the lift! It smells of sick and stale pee. But there's some people I know – Mum, to give just one example – that would get completely out of breath going up ten flights of stairs. I don't! So I know I'm not a slob, and I'm certainly not a glutton. *It is just the way I'm made*, and I refuse to let small-minded, pea-brained pond life such as Marigold Johnson make me self-conscious.

That is what I have always told myself. But oh, that day she really got to me! It's like I'd built up this wall to keep me safe, and she'd gone and brought the whole lot crashing down, leaving me exposed. Like naked, almost. Like a snail brutally torn out of its shell. Now I couldn't pretend any more: it really hurts when someone calls you names.

If Nan had been there, what would she have said?

"Don't you take no notice! You just remember, you've got something girls like that can only dream of… you've got a voice that's going to take you right to the top. Up there with the stars, that's where you'll be! Then she'll be laughing on the other side of her face, you see if she isn't."

But what if Nan were wrong? What if I didn't have a voice?

I knew in my heart that Nan wasn't wrong; I *knew* that I could sing. No one could take that away from me. But no one could make me look like Marigold Johnson, either! And who wanted a rock star the size of an elephant?

I tried so hard to hear Nan again. To hear her old,

cracked voice telling me to have faith, to "Go for it, girl!" But it was no use. She wasn't there, and I couldn't bring her back. Music was all I had left. I turned up the volume until it was almost unbearable, until my head was pounding with the beat and I felt that I was drowning in a crashing sea of sound. At least that way I didn't have to think.

If I could have stayed plugged in I'd have been all right, but Mum came home at six o'clock and I had to crawl back into the world, without my shell. Needless to say, Mum had bumped into Mrs Henson – or, more likely, Mrs Henson had bumped into her.

"What's all this about a headache?" she said. "I never heard of anyone being sent home for a headache. Why couldn't they just give you an aspirin, or something?"

I mumbled that they didn't like to give medication. Mum said, "Sooner send you back to an empty flat."

"They didn't know it was empty. I told them you were here."

Mum looked at me, rather hard. "OK! What did you want to get out of?"

"Nothing," I said. "Nothing!"

"Look, Carmen, just be honest. If it was a maths test, or you hadn't done your homework, I can sympathise. I know what it's like, I've been there! No one's expecting you to turn into some kind of mad boffin. Just don't *lie* to me. All right?"

I said, "Yeah, all right. Sorry."

It seemed easier than going on with the headache thing. Mum's never expected much of me, so not doing homework or avoiding a maths test was no big deal as far as she was concerned. *She* left school without any qualifications; why should I do any better? It would have upset her far more if I'd told her the truth. Not that I would! Not in a million years. I'd have curled up and died sooner than tell Mum.

Indy rang me after tea. I knew she would; I'd been dreading it. I didn't want to talk to her! I wouldn't have minded so much if she'd texted me, but Indy is practically the only person I know that doesn't have a mobile phone. *Or* a computer. It makes life very difficult.

Mum took the phone call. She came back into the sitting room and said, "It's your little friend on the phone. The little plain one." I do *wish* Mum wouldn't refer to Indy as the little plain one! I really hate it when she does that. She knows perfectly well what her name is.

"Well, are you going to speak to her," she said, "or not?"

I dragged myself out into the hall and picked up the phone. "'Lo?"

Indy shrieked, "Carm! What happened? Where did you get to?"

"Hadda headache," I said.

"Cos of Marigold? I knew it was cos of her! Honestly, that girl is just *so* putrefying! I'm glad you told her she was a moron. Everybody's glad! They all reckon she asked for it."

I said, "How does everybody know? Did you tell them?"

"No! It was Connie."

Connie Li; I hadn't realised she was there. Connie is OK. She is definitely *not* a Marigold groupie.

"Carm?" Indy's voice squeaked anxiously down the line. "You haven't let her get to you? Cos all those things she said, about her sister… they're not really true! She hasn't really had professional experience."

"You mean she hasn't appeared in a commercial?"

"Only some stupid thing for local radio. Not telly."

"What about the demo disc?"

"Yeah, well… anyone can make one of those."

I said, "Huh!"

"She isn't any competition," said Indy. "She has a voice like a… I dunno! Fingernails scraping on a blackboard. Yeeeech!"

Indy was trying really hard, but what she said about fingernails just wasn't true. Marigold's sister is chosen every year to sing solo when we do carols. It's not a bad sort of voice. A bit *small*. A bit *tinny*. She couldn't do rock! But obviously some people like it. Anyway, I couldn't care less about Marigold's sister. It was all the other stuff. The stuff that Indy was too kind to mention, or maybe just too embarrassed.

"You've always said not to take any notice of her," said Indy. "So why start now?"

"I'm not," I said. "I don't give a damn." It's amazingly easy to lie when you're on the other end of a telephone. You can almost, even, lie to yourself. "Marigold Johnson is just sewage," I said.

"She is," said Indy. "That's exactly what she is! And we're not the only ones that think so. Lots of people have been going on about her. It's made her really unpopular."

I knew Indy was doing her best to be a good friend and make me feel better, but I hated the thought of everyone knowing what Marigold had said. Everyone talking about it. Feeling sorry for me. *Did you hear what Marigold called Carmen? She called her a fat freak!*

"Dunno what she meant by that last remark, though," said Indy. "D'you?"

I said, "What last remark?" Though in fact I knew perfectly well.

"Fag hag... what she say that for?"

I said, "No idea."

"I thought when people called you a fag hag it meant you were friends with someone that was gay."

I grunted.

"You're not friends with anyone that's gay! Unless she was talking about Josh. Was she talking about Josh? Trying to make out he's a fag?"

I snapped, "Don't use that stupid word!"

"Sorry," said Indy. "Was she trying to make out he's gay?"

I said, "I don't *know*! She's completely mad."

"But what a thing to say! About Josh. I bet she's just jealous, I bet that's what it is, cos she used to fancy him. Probably still does. And just cos he doesn't fancy her—"

"Whatever you do," I said, "don't tell him!"

"I won't," said Indy. "I wouldn't!"

"I s'pose people are *gossiping*?"

"Not about that so much. They're more saying how Marigold got what she deserved… you calling her a vegetable!" Indy giggled. "Someone said she ought to have a new name – she ought to be called *Cabbage*. Then someone said she ought to be a root veg, cos of you telling her to take root, so we're all, like, trying to think of root vegetables, like *Turnip*. Turnip Johnson!"

I said, "Yeah, that would suit her. But *please* don't tell Josh about the other thing. *Please!*"

"I won't," said Indy. "I won't! Don't worry!" She added that in any case it was so stupid it was ridiculous. "No one's going to believe it."

I said, "That's not the point! I don't want him to *know*."

If word got round, it would be all my fault. I should just have kept quiet! I'd done what I always swore I wouldn't: I'd let myself be provoked. I'd insulted

Marigold in front of her groupies, and now she'd gone and dragged Josh into it. He was going to think I'd betrayed him! Why, why, *why* couldn't I have kept my big mouth shut? Just a few weeks earlier, before I'd even known about the Top Spot contest, I'd gone round to Josh's place and we'd written a new song – *How Cool am I?* – and afterwards we'd sat and talked, cos Josh and I do a *lot* of talking, and he'd said he had something he wanted to tell me. And then he'd hesitated, and I said, "Well, go on! What?" and it all came out in a great rush.

"I'm not absolutely certain but it's this feeling I've had for a long time… I think I might be gay!"

I said, "Oh." And then, "Really?" And then, "Gosh." Like something out of Enid Blyton. I gave up reading Enid Blyton when I was about *five*. To make matters worse I then added, "Wow."

Josh said, "Yeah. Wow."

"Well, but I mean…" What did I mean? I didn't mean anything. I was just, like, totally thrown. It's not very often I'm at a loss for words, usually I have too many, but for once I couldn't think of a single thing to say. So I went and said something even stupider than wow, I said, "How do you know?"

"I dunno," said Josh. "It's just something I feel."

"Mm." I nodded. "OK. So…"

He looked at me, rather solemnly. "So how do *you* feel?"

"Me? I feel like – so what? What difference does it make? You're still you. So long as we're not going to fancy the same guys!"

I said that just to show him that I was cool. That now I'd got my head round the idea I was just, like, totally and utterly relaxed.

"You're the only person I've told," said Josh.

"Not even Robert? Not even Damian?"

Josh said, "Specially not Robert or Damian."

They are two boys in our class. They're clever, like Josh. The three of them tend to hang out together.

"Why specially not them?" I said. "Don't you

reckon they'd be OK with it?"

"I guess – yeah! Probably. It's just... I don't particularly want anyone else to know."

"Just me?"

I think that was one of the proudest moments of my life. That Josh had chosen *me*! But I still had to ask him. "Why me and not anybody else?"

He said, "Cos I feel you're someone I can talk to. Maybe the *only* person I can talk to."

"Not even your mum and dad?"

"God, no!" He reared away in horror. "I'm not gonna tell them!"

"Why not?"

"Are you mad? Would you tell your mum?"

I said, "N-no. But I'd tell yours!" Josh's mum and dad are really nice. Really supportive. "You should tell them," I said. "Otherwise you know what'll happen... they'll start teasing you about girlfriends, and it'll just be, like, *so* embarrassing. It's what my mum does about boys. It curls me up! You should tell them now," I said, "so they have time to get used to it. You don't want to spring it on them later."

Josh said he didn't want to spring it on them at all. "There isn't any reason for them to know. There isn't any reason for anyone to know."

Just me. I assured him that I wouldn't breathe a word to a soul, not even Indy, and I snatched up my guitar and started singing the song we'd just written.

How cool am I?
Think about about about a
NICE cube
Think about about about a
NICE cream
Think about a nice dream
Ice dream

Well, it went on for a bit and now I've forgotten the rest of it. But it did seem significant that we'd written it that particular day.

"See?" I said. "How cool am I!"

"I knew you would be," said Josh. "That's why I knew I could tell you."

Everyone needs someone they can tell things to. Josh had told me he was worried cos he thought he might be gay – but I couldn't tell Josh that I was worried cos I thought I might be too fat to be a rock star. I was too ashamed. I didn't have anyone I could tell.

He said, "Promise me you won't say anything!" and I gave him my word. I promised him. He had confided in me in strictest secrecy. He had *trusted* me. And now that hideous hag Marigold had gone and blown it. How had she found out? I hadn't told a single solitary person. It had nearly killed me keeping it from Indy, cos me and Indy tell each other everything, but I hadn't even so much as hinted. I wouldn't do that to Josh!

My only hope was that everyone would be so busy gabbing about how Marigold had called me a fat freak and I'd called her a moron that they'd forget the words she'd yelled at me as I stalked through the door. Maybe Josh would never get to hear of it.

But I knew that he would. School is just like a seething cauldron when it comes to gossip.

CHAPTER THREE

Next day was Wednesday. Only Wednesday! I felt like I had lived through a whole week already. Mum was on early turn. She came breezing into my bedroom while I was still wrapped in the duvet with my eyes gummed shut. She started making noise almost before she even got through the door.

"CAR-MEN!"

I burrowed deeper down the bed. Mum's voice goes all shrill when it gets loud. *Not* what you need, first thing in the morning.

"Carmen, I'm off now. I'll be back about six. OK?"

I mumbled into the duvet.

"OK?" shrieked Mum.

I said, "*Yes.* OK!"

"Right, well, it's time you were up. Come on, get moving!"

Mum tugged at the duvet; I tugged back.

"CAR-MEN!"

"All right, all right!" I poked my head out, and forced my eyes open the merest crack. "I'm coming!"

"Well, just see that you are. I'm pulling back the curtains – " *Whoosh.* Blinding daylight. I quickly screwed my eyes tight shut again. Why did she have to be so brutal? "You've got twenty minutes to get yourself up and out!"

"Yeah, yeah." *Just go away.*

"I'll see you tonight."

Yeah. See you tonight. Now *go*.

She went. I heard her footsteps down the hall; I heard the front door open and bang shut behind her. Within seconds, I had gone back to sleep.

If the telephone hadn't rung, I might have gone on sleeping all day. As it was, it was almost two o'clock. I couldn't believe it! *Two o'clock*. I had been asleep the entire morning.

The telephone went on ringing. I jumped out of bed and went into the hall to look at it, while I decided what to do. To answer or not to answer? *Not*. I didn't want to speak to anyone. But it kept on ringing, like it was determined to get some sort of response, so in the end I gave in and picked it up – and immediately wished I hadn't cos it was Indy again. Indy was one of the last people I wanted to speak to.

"*Carm?*" I held the receiver away from my ear. If Mum's voice goes shrill, Indy's goes all high-pitched and squealy, like a car alarm. "Carm, what's happening? Why aren't you in school?"

Rather sourly I said, "Still gotta headache."

"*Still?*"

I said, "Yeah. Why aren't you in class?"

"I'm going. I just wanted to speak to you – I've borrowed Connie's phone. Carm..."

"What?"

"You know you said not to tell Josh? Well... I think he knows."

My heart did that plummeting thing, like when you're sitting on a plane and there's turbulence and you fall into an air pocket, or whatever it is that planes do. When they *lurch*, and you think your last hour has come.

"*Pleeeeez* don't be mad," begged Indy.

I said, "I'm not mad."

"You sound like you are."

I snapped, "Well, I'm not! I'm just sick of people tittle-tattling. Who was it?"

"I don't know, but Lance S—"

"That *thug?*"

"He was making these really stupid remarks, and Josh was there, so he must have heard, but— What?" She broke off. "Yes, OK. I'm coming! Carm, listen, I'm sorry, I'll have to go. I just w—"

"Don't you ring off!" I screeched.

"I've got to, it's the bell."

"Damn the bell! I want to know what that thug said?"

"I'll tell you tomorrow. You're gonna be here tomorrow, aren't you?"

"I don't know, I don't know! Tell me now."

"Carm, I can't, it's maths, you know what Mr Dearden's like. If—"

"Tell me right this minute," I bawled, "or I won't ever speak to you again!"

There was a pause.

"I mean it! I'm not joking. You either tell me what he said, or—"

"I'll tell you tomorrow," said Indy. She said it in this very dignified tone of voice. No squealing. No car alarms. "I have to go now or I'll be late for class."

"Well, don't bother ringing," I snarled, "cos I won't be answering!"

Whether she heard me or not, I wasn't sure. The phone had gone dead, leaving me in a kind of trembling fury. Fury with Marigold, fury with the Thug; fury with Indy for not telling me, fury with myself for having set the whole thing off. *Answering back to Marigold.* It was asking for trouble. And now I'd gone and brought it down on Josh, as well as myself.

There was only one way to find solace: for the rest of the afternoon I let Urban Legend pound my brain to atoms. Mum always says that I'll damage my hearing if I listen to music that loud. "You'll be deaf by the time you're my age!"

I tell her that lots of rock stars end up with dodgy hearing. "It's part of the price you pay."

That afternoon I couldn't have cared less. I just wanted to deaden my brain. It suddenly felt like my whole life was falling apart.

Round about four o'clock I lugged myself out to the kitchen to forage for food. Breakfast stuff was still on the table, so I ate a bowl of cereal and made some toast, then decided that maybe I should get dressed before Mum arrived back. Just as well I did, cos the doorbell rang. I thought it was probably Mrs Gasbag come to beg a bowl of sugar or a packet of peas. She's always doing that, it drives me nuts, but Mum says we have to be neighbourly. Anyway, it wasn't her, it was Josh. For the second time that day my heart plummeted. *Thunk*, like a sack of cement.

I said, "Oh – hi."

Josh said, "Hi."

And then we both went quiet. And then we both spoke at the same time:

"Did you—"

"Do you—"

"After you," said Josh.

I swallowed. I have *never* been self-conscious with

Josh. Not even right at the beginning, when he picked me instead of Marigold.

"Do you... want-to-come-in?"

It wasn't even my voice! It was like some kind of growl. We went through to the sitting room and stood, awkwardly.

I said, "Mum's still at work."

Josh said, "Ah."

Then we both said, "So—"

"Your turn," I said.

"Yeah. OK! I was just, like... wondering how you were. Indy said you had a headache, she was worried about you. So I said I'd call round after school. I've brought your homework."

No one but Josh would think about bringing *homework*. He held out a sheet of paper. "English and history. I printed it off for you."

I thanked him as graciously as my voice would permit. It was still coming out in a growl.

He said, "I didn't think you'd want to fall behind...

I know they're your best subjects."

"After music."

"Oh. Yeah! Well. After music." He grinned. I tried to grin back, but I couldn't seem to get my lips moving in the right direction. "So… you OK?"

I said, "Yes! I mean… you know... Apart from a headache."

"I heard what happened."

"Before you say anything else—" My tongue suddenly broke loose. The words came babbling out, unstoppable. "I wasn't the one that told them! Lance and Marigold… I didn't say a word! Honestly! I didn't even tell Indy!"

"It's OK," said Josh. "Don't worry about it."

"But I—"

"Carm, it's OK. I told you, don't worry! I can handle it."

"You shouldn't have to handle it! They shouldn't be saying things like that! I just don't see how they f—"

"Carm, for God's sake, will you just SHUT UP!"

I was startled into silence. Josh is such a together person; he almost never shouts or loses his cool.

"I don't want to talk about it, OK?"

I swallowed. "OK."

"I didn't come here to talk about me, I came to talk about you."

Guardedly, I said, "What about me?"

"Why you're not at school."

"You know why I'm not at school! I've got this headache."

"Yeah, you said."

"It's like a migraine. It's really really—"

"Carmen, stop it!" I thought for a moment he was going to shake me. That startled me even more. It was so not Josh! We didn't treat each other like that. "What's happened to you? Why have you suddenly let them get to you? They're not worth it! People like Marigold Johnson… they're just body fascists. Nothing up here." He tapped his head. "Completely empty. All they think about is looks."

I knew that Josh, like Indy, was only trying to help, but it just made me feel even more humiliated than I had before. I'd always been so determined not to feel ashamed of my own body that *size* wasn't something I'd ever discussed. Not even with Indy. We'd never had girly-type conversations with me moaning about spare tyres and Indy fretting over lack of boobs. We'd always pretended we were just ordinary, regular, girl-shaped girls. That is, *I'd* pretended. Indy had just been kind and humoured me.

When I went shopping for clothes and Josh came along and chose brilliant, clever tops that flattered me, of course I knew that he was looking at my bum and thinking, *How can we cover that up?* but he didn't ever say so. *I* didn't ever say so. Not even in joke, like, "Ooh, hide the big fat bum!" I suppose I had this idea that if neither of us ever mentioned it, it would mean that he hadn't really noticed. Which is totally and utterly pathetic, cos how could he not?

"There's only one way to deal with them," said

Josh. "You just have to ignore them."

I muttered, "I've been ignoring them."

"So go on ignoring them!"

He thought it was that easy?

"Just come back and make like nothing ever happened, and it'll all blow over. Honestly! I promise! People *like* you. They don't like Marigold. But you're funny and sharp and you stick up for yourself. People admire you for that. They're *glad* you slagged her off. They reckon it was about time."

I thought, *Yes, and look where it got me. Look where it got both of us.*

"Just come back," said Josh.

I pursed my lips.

"The longer you leave it, the harder it's going to get. If you came back tomorrow—"

"Dunno if I'm gonna come back at all."

"*What?*"

"I said, I don't know if I'm going to come back at all."

"Don't be daft! You'll have to, sooner or later."

"Why?"

"They'll make you."

"They can't. Not if I refuse. Not unless they *drag* me, and then they'd have to keep me in chains."

"That's ridiculous!"

"No, it isn't."

"Course it is! You're being silly. They'd just take you into care, or put you in an institution, or something."

"Think that'd bother me?"

"Well, it should!"

"Well, it doesn't."

I could see that I was exasperating him. I didn't want to; I just didn't seem able to stop myself. What with Indy, and now Josh, I was beginning to feel distinctly got at.

"What about the contest?" said Josh. "They won't let you enter if you're not at school."

"So?"

"So we've written the song! We've chosen your outfit. You can't back out now!"

If there's one thing I really cannot stand, it's being pushed around. Specially when I know, deep inside myself, that the person who's doing the pushing is right. That makes me even madder than when they're wrong. That makes me *really* resentful.

I gave Josh one of my looks. I have this look which says, as plain as can be, BACK OFF. Most people, when I give them the look, immediately shut up. Josh just went motoring on, regardless. He said, "Carm, come on! You owe it to us... me and Indy. We're rooting for you! So are loads of other people. You owe it to them, as well. You owe it to your nan!"

I practically screamed it at him: "Don't you bring my nan into it!"

Still he didn't back off. "You know what she'd say... she'd say you were letting yourself down." I felt my face turn slowly crimson. "Letting her down, as well. *Haven't got what it takes.*"

I snarled, "You shut up!"

"I won't shut up. How can you be such a coward?"

He had some nerve! "Talk about *me* being a coward! What about you? Haven't even got the bottle to come out to your own mum and dad!"

I shouldn't have said it. It was mean, turning on Josh when all he was trying to do was help me.

Stiffly, he said, "We've already been through that."

Even now I couldn't stop myself. I snapped, "Not properly, we haven't! All you said was you didn't want them to know. What you actually meant was, you were too scared to tell them, and that is just *pathetic*. Too scared to tell your own mum and dad! Then you dare to come round here and start on at *me*."

Josh said, "I'm not starting on at you."

"Well, ha ha, that's very funny, cos it's certainly what it sounds like!"

"Yeah? Well, you know what? I wish I'd never bothered!"

"You and me both!"

We stood there, glaring at each other. Speaking personally, if I'd been Josh I'd have walked out right there and then, but I guess Josh is a nicer person than I am. He said, "Oh look, for goodness sake, this is really stupid! If we can't even t—"

"*Go away!*" I screamed it at him. "I'm sick of being lectured, and especially by you!"

This time, he finally got the message. I guess I'd gone just a bit too far, even for Josh. Coldly, he said, "If that's the way you want it."

"It is!"

"OK!"

I followed him back out into the hall and stood, simmering, waiting for him to go.

"At least I'm not bunking off school," he said.

He didn't even slam the door behind him. I would have done.

Needless to say, the minute he'd gone I collapsed like a squashed meringue. Mum's always said that one of these days my tongue will get the better of me. "Just can't learn to control it, can you?" I could even hear Nan rebuking me. "Well, that's it, girl! You've really gone and done it this time."

I'd bawled at Indy, now I'd bawled at Josh. But it was his own fault! He shouldn't have brought Nan into it. He knew she was the only person in my entire life who'd ever really, truly loved me. He knew how much I missed her.

Memories of Nan came flooding over me and plunged me into even deeper depths of misery. When Mum came home at six o'clock she was considerably annoyed to find that last night's dinner dishes, plus this morning's breakfast stuff, were still mouldering unwashed in the sink, and the pizza which apparently (so she said) I was supposed to have taken out of the freezer and put in the oven was still in the freezer, and the oven hadn't even been turned on, and for crying out loud, Carmen, you haven't done a single solitary thing!

I told her that I had in fact been doing my

homework, and waved Josh's print-out at her to prove it. It wouldn't have cut any ice with Mum even if it had been true. She went on at some length about how she had been working for eight hours straight, and the least she deserved was to find dinner ready and waiting for her when she got back. I guess she had a point. One way or another, it was a pretty horrible kind of evening.

CHAPTER FOUR

Mum was on late turn next day, so I had to get up and get dressed and make like I was going to school. While I was munching cereal in the kitchen, her mobile started squawking. She yelled at me from the bathroom. "Carmen, get that for me!" So I picked it up and found it was a text message from school, alerting

Mum to the fact that I hadn't been there yesterday. I'd forgotten they did that. Phew! Lucky for me I'd got there first. I deleted it immediately.

"Who was it?" said Mum.

I told her it was someone trying to sell something.

Mum said, "Sell what?"

"Didn't ask."

"Well, in future I would like to *know*," said Mum. "It could have been a free kitchen. How do you know it wasn't a free kitchen?"

I said, "It wasn't a free anything. It was just rubbish." I grabbed my bag and made for the door. "I gotta go, I'll be late!"

I caught the bus at the usual stop, but instead of getting off at Ravenspark Road I stayed on till we reached the shopping centre. I wasn't going back to that school again *ever*. Of course I knew they would come for me. I'd be hunted down like a criminal and dragged off in chains, or more likely handcuffs. I'd heard of people being brought back to school by the police. But they couldn't make me stay there! I'd just keep running off until in the end they'd be forced to send me somewhere else. Either that, or lock me up. Whichever. I didn't care! Sooner be behind bars than have to suffer Marigold Johnson and her gang of sniggering morons every day.

"*That fat freak! What's she think she's gonna do?*"

The words still rang in my ears. I had the feeling that everyone was staring at me. *Ooh, look! Fat!* Body fascists, that's what Josh had called them. *You're the wrong size, you're the wrong shape! Yeeeurgh, bluuurgh, don't want her joining the club!*

Thinking of Josh, as I went into the shopping centre, made me feel bad all over again. He and Indy were my two best friends, and I'd upset both of them. Josh had trusted me with his secret. He'd confided in me what he wouldn't even confide in his mum and dad, and I knew how hard it must have been for him. He is such a very *private* sort of person. He doesn't just blurt things out like I do. He'd probably been screwing up his courage for weeks before finally bringing himself to tell me. How could I have been so mean as to fling it back in his face?

And how could I have snarled at Indy? Threatening never to talk to her again! Indy and I had been friends since our very first day in Year 7. She was the only black girl, I was the only fat girl, and I guess we drifted together for comfort. Nobody else, right at the beginning, seemed to want to know us. Indy and her mum had just moved from London, and out of all my special gang at juniors I was the only one that got sent to Ravenspark. My best mate Janey was supposed to be coming with me, but at the last minute her mum and dad had gone off to live in Australia, leaving me on my own. *Marigold* had been at juniors, but she didn't want to know me any more than I wanted to know her. Me and Indy were always going to be outsiders. Most everyone else got sucked into Marigold's orbit before even the first week was out.

Fortunately, as it happened, me and Indy hit it off

from the word go. We both came from single parent families, which was an immediate bond. And we both utterly despised Marigold Johnson, which was another. I love Indy! She is really funny and scatty. She has a little brother who is even scattier. He gives us lots of laughs, like when he asked his mum to buy a second fish tank so his fish could go on holiday. Actually, I thought that was just so sweet! He was only six years old, and he really cared about his fish.

Nan used to like Indy. She said, "That girl has a happy face." Mum, on the other hand, always makes me grind my teeth. She says it's "so amusing" to see us together, what with me being so huge and Indy being so tiny. Well, she doesn't actually say huge; what she says is *big*. But that is just a polite word for fat.

Another thing she says, though not in so many words, is "How come a boy like Josh" – meaning a boy who could have his pick of any girl he chose – "goes round with someone like you?" Not even Mum would be horrid enough to actually say it to my face, but I know that is what she thinks. She occasionally lets slip these remarks. She is so beautiful and glamorous herself that she considers it a total waste, like for instance if Darrin O'Shea from Urban Legend were to hang out with – oh, I don't know! Some ancient old bag of a politician, maybe. Why not have a girlfriend as gorgeous as he is?

It's what Marigold thought, and the reason she got so insanely jealous, cos how could someone like Josh prefer a wobbly jelly to a prom queen like her?

What Mum has never been able to get her head round, though I've told her over and over, is that Josh is not my boyfriend, he is just my *friend.* We confide in each other and look out for each other and support each other when things go wrong, like when Josh's cat went missing and I helped him look for her, and went round the streets sticking notices on lamp posts, and did my best to cheer him up when he thought he was never going to see her again. Like when Nan died, and it was Josh who was there for me. Indy was, too, except she lives miles away, while Josh is just ten minutes down the road. I cried buckets all over him. Not over *Mum*; I didn't shed a tear, hardly, in front of Mum. Mum didn't shed a tear, either, cos of being scared she'd make her mascara run. Well, no, I'm being unfair, she did cry a little bit, when she first got back from the hospital, just not in public when she had her make-up on.

Mum never loved Nan the way I did; sometimes I used to think she almost resented her coming to live with us. They certainly didn't always see eye to eye, in fact they used to fall out quite a lot, mainly over me. Mum used to say that Nan automatically took my side whenever we had an argument, while Nan said Mum did nothing but carp and criticise. She always used to stick up for me, especially when Mum went on about my weight.

"Just leave the girl alone! We can't all go round looking like bits of string… wouldn't want to, neither. Some of us like a bit of flesh on our bones."

It used to make Mum so mad! She accuses me of having a sharp tongue, but if I do it's her I get it from. It's true I am not a doormat; I don't believe in just lying down and letting myself get trampled on by the Marigold Johnsons of this world. But I am not a bad sort of person. I really am not! I had never *ever* yelled at Josh or Indy before. It was all the fault of that hideous Marigold. She had turned me into a right cow.

I tramped on, round the shopping centre, trying to find something interesting to do. I was just about to go into HMV and check whether there was anything by Urban Legend that I hadn't got (which I knew there wouldn't be) when my mobile started up. I thought, *I am not going to answer it!* But it turned out to be a text message from Josh. *R U coming in 2day?* I immediately texted back: *No I told U.* So then he wants to know, *Why not?* And I tell him, *U no why not.* So then he says, *UR missing maths* and I tell him, *Good* (because I hate maths) and for just a few minutes it makes me feel quite triumphant. Yay! I'm missing maths! I'm walking round the shopping centre while everyone else is stuck in a dreary classroom listening to Mr Fenwick drone on about equations. Best of all, Josh hasn't given up on me.

Made bold by a sudden mad burst of enthusiasm I go waltzing into HMV and begin happily browsing, picking things up and putting them down, until I notice someone watching me and immediately become self-conscious and go rushing back out into the shopping centre and walking furiously in no particular direction.

A couple of policemen are strolling past. They give me these really suspicious looks, like "What is that girl doing here?" and "Why isn't she in school?" but I stare back boldly and they go on their way, leaving me alone. It's a good thing we don't have to wear much in the way of uniforms at Ravenspark, specially in summer. Just black trousers and a white top. Nobody's going to know which school I go to, unless I have the misfortune to bump into someone like Mrs Gasbag – or Mum.

The thought of bumping into Mum makes me go

scuttling like a frightened hen down to the far end of the shopping centre. Mum works in the High Street so she's not very likely to be around, especially at this time of day, but on the whole it seems best not to take any chances. She'd do her nut if she discovered I wasn't in school again.

I have heard that some shopping centres are really fun places, where you can easily spend an entire day without ever getting bored or running out of things to do. Ours is not like that. It is called the Bosworth Centre, which is a very dreary name for a very dreary place, especially when you don't have any money. But I didn't dare go home before my usual time in case of running into Gasbag. I swear that woman spends her life peering through the letter box, waiting to spy on me.

At lunch time I bought a bag of crisps and an apple and sat and munched in a corner, keeping an eye open for Mum, or Gasbag, or anyone else that might recognise me. After lunch I went into Primark and wandered up and down the aisles, gazing at stuff, until I felt that I was being watched again, probably by a big beefy store detective who'd haul me off to be strip searched before I even had a chance to turn my pockets out and show him they were empty.

I left Primark and scuttled next door into Superdrug. In Superdrug they had bins full of stuff just asking to be nicked. So I nicked some. For absolutely no reason at all, except for something to do. It wasn't even like it was something I wanted. I mean, camomile wipes! What was I going to do with those, for heaven's sake? They had cotton wool balls in another bin, and I'd have nicked some of them, as well, if I'd been brave enough. It wasn't conscience that stopped me, but fear of being arrested. Maybe Josh was right, and I really was a coward.

I slid out of Superdrug and into the Choc Shop, which is right next door. They have these ultra gollopy delish chox in the Choc Shop. Handmade, with yummy gooey fillings. Mum never buys any as they are a)

expensive and b) *fattening*. But just now and again, Nan used to treat us. Her and me. We'd have gollopy delish chox together, sitting at one of the little tables, with Nan sipping a big frothy cappuccino and me slurping at one of their special fizzy bubble drinks, all pink and sweet and zingy. That was before Nan's arthritis became so bad she hardly ever left the flat. It seemed like such a long time since Nan and me had had fun together.

I dithered in the doorway, trying to get up the nerve to do a quick snatch and grab. I fantasised what Nan might say. *Go for it, girl!* She was wicked, was Nan; she could egg you on. But I didn't think even Nan would encourage me to shoplift.

I walked out empty-handed, feeling a bit defiant. If Nan wouldn't encourage me to shoplift, I bet she wouldn't encourage me to get up in front of Marigold Johnson and her cronies and sing *Star Crazy Me* and run the risk of being jeered at, either. It's not what she would want! She was always quick to jump to my defence, like if Mum made one of her remarks.

I remembered once when we'd been watching *The Wizard of Oz* – which I must have seen about a dozen times – and I was singing *Somewhere Over the Rainbow*, giving it all I'd got, Nan clapped her hands and cried, "You'll be a second Judy Garland, one of these days!"

Judy Garland is the name of the person who played Dorothy in the movie. I have to admit, when I was younger I did model myself on her, just a little bit. Nan loved it, as Judy Garland was possibly her all-time favourite singer. Anyway, while I was still basking in Nan's praise, Mum had to go and ruin everything by saying rather pointedly, with a look at me, that *Judy Garland* had a lot of problems with her weight.

"She got really fat."

Nan hit back, quick as a flash: "Yes, and everybody loved her!"

And I bet nobody called *her* a fat freak. Josh wasn't being fair! He had no idea what it was like, constantly having to remind yourself, *I will not be ashamed of my own body.* But at the same time always, always being aware that you weren't stick thin and beautiful. That all the stick thin beautiful people were looking at you and sniggering. Or, even worse, feeling sorry for you. I was **NOT GOING TO GET UP ON THAT STAGE AND BE FELT SORRY FOR.** No way!

I went up to the next floor on one of the escalators. Not that there was anything up there, just a load more boring shops. I mean *really* boring shops. Middle-aged women shops. All full of cardigans and clumpy shoes and raincoats. For a while I slobbed around in Smith's, reading magazines, until I got that feeling again that I was being watched. I think it's what they call *paranoia.* Means you think everyone's out to get you. It's how I felt, that day in the shopping centre.

I went back down to the ground floor and wandered aimlessly until I came to Bean Bags, which is one of the few really quality shops in the Bosworth Centre. I couldn't resist going in there, even though most of their stuff is way beyond my reach. It's where we'd got all my cool, rock-chick stuff for the talent contest. The designer-label T-shirt, the silver chain, the stars to put in my hair. *Stars for a star, cos that's what you're going to be!*

Memories came flooding back... me and Josh and Indy, all bubbly and excited. Now I was on my own, full of misery and self-pity. My beautiful T-shirt, that I wasn't going to wear! Suddenly I had this desperate urge to weep and scream and had to go out, very quickly, and start furiously walking again until I had calmed down.

At the entrance to the pedestrian underpass a girl was singing, accompanying herself on a guitar. I stopped for a bit, to listen. She was one of those tall, willowy types that make me mad with envy. She had this gorgeous, foamy red hair and was wearing long thin jeans and a skimpy top that I wouldn't even dare to think about. On the other hand she couldn't play the guitar any better than I could, or even as well. It was all just plinking and plonking. Plus, for heaven's sake, she was *ruining* one of my favourite songs. She was trying to do a track from the latest album, *Love Heart*, by Topaze. God, it was an insult!

I felt like wrenching the guitar away from her and banging her on the head with it. But then she caught my eye and smiled at me, and I forced myself to smile back. She wasn't to know that Topaze happens to be one of the singers I most worship and adore in the whole wide world. What is more, *she actually went to my school.* How cool is that?

In spite of forcing myself to smile, I felt that I might scream or go mad if I stayed listening any longer while this girl-without-any-voice massacred a perfectly good song. At the same time, I couldn't help feeling a bit glad that she didn't have a voice as it saved me being totally eaten up with hideous jealousy. She had the hair, she had the face, she had the figure – but she still couldn't sing!

It was almost half past three by now, so I reckoned it would be safe to catch a bus and go home. When I got there Old Gasbag was in the lobby, waiting for the lift. She said, "You're back early." I ignored her, and headed for the stairs.

When Mum came in, I had not only done the washing-up but had dinner all ready and waiting. I didn't know what she'd planned for us, so I just took stuff out of the freezer and dumped it in the oven. I thought, *If she dares say anything, I'll throw it at her.* But she seemed surprised, and pleased, and said that it made a nice change being able to get back and put her feet up for once. And then she had to go and ruin everything, which is what she does *all the time*, by saying rather sharply, "I hope you were in school today?"

I said, "What do you think?"

Mum said, "Sometimes, with you, I don't know what to think. You know I could end up in prison, don't you? It's the parents that are held responsible. I'd be the one to be shut away, not you."

I told her that was just a myth, but she insisted it was true. "They could lock me up!"

I said, "They haven't got room to lock people up any more. They're already full to overflowing."

"That's beside the point!" snapped Mum. "I could still get a criminal record."

What with Mum fretting over criminal records, and me sunk into deepest gloom, we passed another happy evening together. Mum wanted to know why I wasn't doing my homework – like she'd ever bothered about homework before – so I had to pretend I'd already done it.

She said, "Huh! That must be a first."

Shows how much she knows. I have always been *very good* about doing my homework. Mum has never shown the least bit of interest in what goes on at school, or what I might be achieving. It was the reason I had never bothered to tell her about the Top Spot contest; she'd only have made one of her remarks.

I fell asleep almost the minute I got into bed, exhausted from all my endless walking round the shopping centre. Also from boredom. Boredom, I have discovered, wears you out. So does being miserable and feeling sorry for yourself. It is very unlike me to feel sorry for myself. Nan once said that I was a feisty sort of person, meaning that I wouldn't ever just give up, or go down without a fight.

I thought of this when I woke up at four o'clock in the morning and couldn't get back to sleep again. I was doing exactly what Nan always said I wouldn't do: I was giving up without a fight. It made me feel ashamed of myself. How could I let Nan down like that? She'd always had such faith in me. She used to say there'd come a day when Mum would be so proud she'd tell everyone she met: "Carmen Bell is my daughter!" Mum never believed her, of course. She didn't actually say "Don't make me laugh" but you could tell that's what she was thinking. You can always tell what Mum is thinking; she never makes any attempt to cover it up. Nan just used to shake her head. "You mark my words, that girl's got what it takes."

I hadn't had what it takes when I was wandering

round the shopping centre. If I wasn't going to go back to school – which I *wasn't* – then I had to do something positive. Something that would make Nan applaud and say, "That's my girl!"

I knew what I would do: I would take my guitar and I would go out there and sing. If the girl with red hair could do it, why not me? I may not be thin as a twig, but I do have a good voice. Far better than hers! I am aware that this sounds like showing off, but it just happens to be true. I *know* that I can sing! It is the only thing I am ever tempted to boast about.

"And why not? Make the most of what you've got, that's my motto!"

Nan's voice in my ear. Even after all this time, just now and again, she still spoke to me. I immediately felt buoyed up and – well, *feisty*. I didn't even try to go back to sleep but lay awake eagerly planning what I was going to sing and where I was going to do it. Not in the shopping centre; that would be asking for trouble. Sooner or later someone would come along who recognised me. If not Mum or Mrs Gasbag, then other people that lived in the flats.

The best place would be down Sheepscombe, the other end of town, near the bus garage. There's a big Tesco there, and a church, with a church hall that's used for Bingo, and a Marks & Spencer and a Boots, plus a load of sheltered housing for old people and a big block of flats for posh people. But nobody who lives up our end would be likely to go there.

I thought probably it would be best if I didn't sing my usual sort of stuff as rock is quite loud and I wouldn't want the police coming and arresting me for making a public nuisance of myself. I decided that I would sing some of Nan's show songs that she loved so much. *Over the Rainbow*, and stuff like that. Nan was really into her musicals – she used to play them over and over. *Oklahoma, West Side Story, My Fair Lady*… thanks to Nan, I knew them all! Old people enjoy that sort of thing, whereas they don't really approve of rock. Nan did, but Nan was different from most old people. I reckoned the ones that lived in the sheltered housing would prefer something a bit quieter, and probably the posh people would, too. If they liked what I did, they might even shower money on me!

But even if they didn't, and I came home empty-handed, it would still be a valuable experience. Probably far more valuable, if you think about it – for a future rock star, that is – than being at school. I felt that Nan would approve!

CHAPTER FIVE

Mum seemed to think it odd, next morning, that I was taking my guitar with me. She said, "What's that for?"

I said, "I'm playing it."

Fortunately she didn't ask me why, or where, which meant I didn't have to make anything up. So far I hadn't told her *one single untruth.* I felt virtuous about that, because at least she couldn't accuse me of lying.

She was in quite a good mood that morning and asked me if I'd like a lift in to school. "I'm not on till ten, but I can leave a bit earlier."

I got in a panic at that and quickly said it was OK, I was quite happy going by bus.

"It's no problem," said Mum. "I might take the opportunity to do a bit of shopping."

The best laid plans of mice and men, as Nan used to chortle when things went wrong. They go *agley*. In other words, they fall to pieces, which is what mine did that morning. Mum *insisted* on giving me a lift almost to the very gates of the school. I reckon now she wanted to make sure I got there; at the time I was naïve enough to believe she was just trying to say thank you for all my hard work the night before. All the washing-up, and dinner on the table.

Well, ha ha, all *her* best laid plans went agley, as well. Ravenspark Road is part of the one-way system

and she had to let me out at the top, so as soon as she'd driven off I simply turned round and headed back to the bus stop, praying I wouldn't bump into anyone from school, and especially not Indy or Josh. I didn't, as it happened, but it was quite nerve-racking at one point when I had to dive down a side road and lurk behind a lamp post to avoid three of the kids from my class. One of them was this girl called Abi Walters who's a bosom buddy of Marigold. She was shrieking and showing off, and the other two were encouraging her. I didn't know what she was showing off about, but once in the past she'd had everyone in stitches pretending to be me, doing what she called her "wobble walk". Seeing her that morning just made me all the more determined never, *ever* to go back.

It was quarter to ten when I got off the bus at Sheepscombe. There were quite a lot of people about, but no kids cos they were all in school. I was glad about that. I didn't want kids; they weren't the ones I was singing for. They weren't the ones I was *dressed* for. I had gone through my wardrobe (what there is of it) and carefully picked out clothes which I thought old people – and posh people – would approve of. No shorty tops showing my midriff. No miniskirts. Instead, I chose an ordinary baggy T-shirt (no rude logos) and a long floaty skirt, dark red, in tiers. I carried them with me in my schoolbag and changed in the loo in Tesco. They even had a long mirror in there so I could inspect myself. Marigold would have sneered, but you have to dress for the occasion. Nan always loved my long floaty skirt, and she was the one I was singing for.

Down by the street market, opposite Marks & Spencer, there's a paved area, with flowering shrubs and wooden benches, where old people sit and chat. I thought that would be a good place to position myself, so I took up a stand just by the entrance and put down my little tin bowl that I had brought with me. The bowl had belonged to Nan's dog, Fluffy, that she had had when she first came to live with us. Mum had hated poor Fluffy cos she was old and starting to get a bit smelly, but Nan had loved her, so I had, too. For Nan's sake, really. I reckoned her drinking bowl might bring me luck.

I was so nervous before I began that my throat closed up and I had visions of standing there, totally dumb, just blowing out bubbles of air. But then, lo and behold! A miracle occurred. The minute I played the first few chords I felt my voice come surging up inside me like a great tidal wave, and I knew that all I had to do was just open my mouth and *sing*. I think it took some of the old people by surprise! I saw heads jerk up and turn in my direction. But once they realised what was going on they seemed to enjoy it, cos I soon had quite a crowd, all smiling and nodding, and sometimes even trying to sing along (which I did my best not to mind).

I gave it everything I'd got, in case Nan was up there somewhere, listening. I did so want her to be proud of me! I sang all her old favourites, in my best Judy Garland voice. Full-throated, flat out. The old people just loved it! After a couple of hours my tin doggy bowl was full almost to overflowing, and I decided I could afford to take a bit of a break and even buy myself a sandwich. After all, I had earned it! I had come by it honestly, and felt that I deserved every penny of it. Far more satisfying than nicking stuff out of Superdrug.

At one o'clock I wandered back and took up my position again. I figured by now there would be a whole new bunch of people out there. Earlier on, before I'd had my lunch break, I'd noticed an old lady standing listening. I mean, there were lots of old ladies, but the reason I noticed this one in particular is that she stood out from the rest. She had this *look*, like she was someone to be reckoned with. She was dressed to kill, in some sort of silk outfit, which you could just tell had cost a fortune. And her face was all made up, to go with it. Blusher and mascara and bright red lipstick. Even her nails were red. She'd stayed for a few songs, then gone off across the square towards the shops. She didn't put anything in the doggie bowl, so I thought perhaps she wasn't impressed. Either that, or she was just plain mean.

But round about two thirty she appeared again, and this time she came up and spoke to me. "You're still at it."

Yup! I was still at it. Don't say she was going to have a go at me… *You're too young to be doing this, why aren't you at school, you're breaking the law,* etc. etc. You can just bet there'll always be *some* law you're breaking.

"How long have you been here?"

Guardedly I said, "Since about ten o'clock."

"Ten o'clock? Singing all this time?"

I muttered that I had had a break for lunch.

"All the same… it's far too long. You need to rest your voice."

I told her that I couldn't afford to. Coins were still pattering into my bowl. I didn't want to give up before I had to!

"*There.*" The old lady opened her purse and took

out – gulp! – a five-pound note. She placed it in the bowl, beneath a pile of coins to keep it from flying off. "Now you can afford to. Let me invite you for a cup of tea."

I nearly said that I don't drink tea, but it would have seemed ungracious after what she'd just done; and in any case, I must admit, I was a bit curious. Why should this posh old woman with her silk dress and her designer bag want to have tea with a nobody like me?

"Come!" She made this imperious gesture, wafting her hand like the Queen. "I'm just over there, in the flats."

I wouldn't have gone with her if she'd been a man; I'm not stupid. I probably wouldn't have gone if she'd been younger. But she was really ancient and I couldn't honestly imagine she was going to poison me or anything, so I picked up my bowl and the money, slung my guitar over my shoulder, and followed her across the road to her block. Oakwood Court. Classy!

She had a flat on the ground floor. It was a bit

different from the one me and Mum lived in. For a start it was colour-coordinated. *All green.* Lime green paper on the walls, dark green carpet on the floor; pale green sofa, pale green chairs. As well as being green, it was what I would call *fussy*. Bits and pieces everywhere. Ornaments and bowls of flowers; lamps in strange shapes, with weird dangling lampshades, and lots of little tables dotted all about. The main room was huge. There was a grand piano in one corner (white, not green) and every single bit of wall space was covered in big glossy photographs and posters.

I wondered who this woman was. She had to be *someone*; ordinary people don't live like that.

She told me to take a seat while she made us a cup of tea. "Do you drink tea? I have Earl Grey or herbal."

I asked her if she had a Coke, but she said no; Coke was bad for you.

"I'll do you a peppermint tea. I think you'll find it very refreshing."

While she was out of the room I took the

opportunity to examine some of the photographs and posters. The photographs mostly seemed to be of the same person, starting off young and gradually getting older. In some she was dressed up like for a performance on stage; others were studio portraits. (I think that is what they are known as.) All very dead glamorous, though she wasn't ever pretty; and in lots of them she was wearing *fur*. I hate when people wear fur!

The posters were theatrical ones, advertising operas. *La Bohème* and *La Traviata* and stuff. Then there were the names of singers, and one name which appeared in all of them: Liliana Pruszynski. So I guessed that this weird old woman must once have been famous, which accounted for the way she dressed, and the way she spoke – terribly grand and sure of herself.

I went back and peered more closely at the photographs, and in some of the later ones I could just about see the resemblance – she hadn't yet become prunelike and withered. But definitely it was the same old woman.

I heard her returning with the tea and hastily perched myself on the edge of one of the pale green chairs.

"There you are… peppermint tea. Made with fresh-picked mint."

It had *leaves* floating in it. I wondered what I was supposed to do with them.

"Give them a few minutes, then just take them out and put them in the bowl. Have you not had mint tea before? It's a good habit. You can grow the mint yourself – indoors, in a pot, if you have no garden. You should ask your mother to get some."

Yeah, I could just picture Mum's face if I suggested we started drinking peppermint tea! Come under the heading of "cranky", that would. Mum's into her tea in a big way. She likes it deep dark brown and bitter. Horrible, if you ask me, but it's what she's used to.

"So, my dear…" The old woman settled herself in the chair opposite. The chair was so big, and she was so small, she practically disappeared. "Why are you not in school?"

I thought, *Here we go.* Carelessly, I said, "It's half term."

"Already?"

"Yup." I nodded. "We have two weeks."

Terrible how the lies can just pour out of you. But come Monday it *would* be half term, so it wasn't such a big lie as all that. In any case, what business was it of hers?

"Which school do you go to? It can't be Holy Cross, I know they're not on half term yet. It must be Ravenspark."

I toyed for a moment with the idea of making up a name, but I wasn't quick enough. By the time I'd got my brain into gear, she was off again. "I understand you're going to be putting on some kind of talent contest later in the term. For aspiring pop stars?"

She cocked an eyebrow at me. I muttered, "Yeah." How did she know about it?

She smiled, as if reading my thoughts. "Believe it or not, I was asked to be one of the judges, but oh, my dear, what do I know of pop music? It's for the young. Like you! I take it you'll be entering?"

"Mm-mm." I shook my head.

"No? Why ever not? I would have thought it was right up your street."

I didn't say anything to that; I didn't want to talk about the talent contest. I busied myself fishing leaves out of my cup and flobbing them into a dinky little green bowl. Everything was green. The cups were green. The *tea* was green.

"You do have a very good voice, you know." She leaned forward and ever so delicately picked up her tea cup. She had a lot of style, in spite of being so ancient. "Well, you obviously do know, don't you? How could you avoid knowing? No one has a voice of that quality without realising they've been given a very special gift."

That melted me, I have to admit. But then she had to go and blow it.

"What you may not realise, however..." She wagged an old, gnarled finger at me. On the finger was a massive ring with a gleaming green stone. Emerald, I guess. "What you may not realise is that an instrument such as yours needs nurturing. You should treat it with respect. A voice is like a delicate bloom – like the finest crystal. You misuse it at your peril!"

She seemed to expect me to say something, but I didn't know what to say cos I hadn't the faintest idea what she was talking about. Just that she seemed to be having a go at me.

"You cannot simply blast out at full volume for hours on end as if you're some market trader selling cabbages!"

I resented that. What's wrong with market traders? I didn't see she had any call to get all snobby.

"Surely, my dear, you can understand my concern?" She peered at me out of strangely bright, birdlike eyes. "You're putting your voice under tremendous pressure!"

Somewhat annoyed, I said, "I'm not putting it under pressure. It's just the way I sing."

"Well, it shouldn't be! You'll do permanent damage if you carry on like that."

Now she was really starting to annoy me. It was *my* voice; I knew what was right for it. I said, "I've been singing that way ever since I can remember. It hasn't done it any harm."

"Not yet, maybe. But if you continue singing full out, without any kind of training—"

"Judy Garland sang flat out!" It was one of the things I knew about her. I knew quite a lot, as a matter of fact; I'd once watched a programme with Nan: *Judy Garland the Legend*. "She was famous for always giving her best."

"Yes, and she had great problems with her voice as she grew older. Take it from me! I know what I'm talking about. You can still give of your best without straining your vocal chords. It's a question of technique... I could teach you, if you wanted."

I knew I ought to be gracious, and thank her very kindly, but sometimes I get embarrassed when people offer to do things for me – specially when I'm not quite sure what it is they're offering. I mean... Mum couldn't afford for me to have singing lessons!

I mumbled that that was all right; I wasn't aiming to be an opera singer. Maybe – through embarrassment – I said *opera* in a sneery kind of way, cos she raised both her pencilled eyebrows into her wrinkly old forehead and said, "So for any other kind of singer it doesn't matter if they ruin their voice? Is that what you're telling me? But surely a singer is a singer no matter what! Or maybe you consider your sort of singing to be in some way inferior? In other words, as far as you're concerned, the voice is of no importance?"

That wasn't what I was saying! How dare she put words in my mouth? I gulped down the rest of my minty tea and shoved the cup back on the tray. Then I stood up and grabbed my guitar.

"Oh," she said, "are you leaving now?"

"Gotta get back," I said. "Gotta get Mum's dinner."

"Well, think about what I said."

As I made for the door I stopped and looked again at one of the photos. "Is that you?" I said. "Are you Liliana…" I hesitated.

"Pruszynski." *Pru-shinsky.* "Born plain Lilian Banks, in Manchester. Pruszynski is my married name. You can call me Mrs P."

Why should she think I wanted to call her anything? It wasn't likely I'd be seeing her again.

"Thank you for the tea," I said.

"Thank *you,*" she said. "Hearing you sing was a pleasure."

It's funny, cos she was just an ancient old woman, but when she said that it gave me a real buzz. She'd obviously been someone, in her time; she knew what she was talking about. I *did* have a voice! I *could* become a star!

I strode back across the paved area, past the flowering shrubs and the benches full of old people, with my guitar slung over my shoulder, feeling that even if I wasn't yet a star, I was a professional. I'd made money! I'd made at least twelve pounds.

I decided that before catching the bus home I'd go into Marks & Spencer and see if I could find something nice for Mum. Something in the food department. She hardly ever buys stuff from M&S cos she says it's too expensive, but she really does like it; and for some reason I suddenly had this great feeling of fondness for her and wanted to make her happy. I dunno! Maybe it was guilt. Anyway, I bought a big fruit tart covered in cherries and grapes, and tiny little bits of orange and melon. I thought she'd enjoy that. She couldn't say that fruit tart was fattening. I mean, *fruit*... it's supposed to be good for you.

While I was waiting for Mum to come in I had a text message. It was from Josh, telling me that he was off to Malta to visit his grandparents. He often does that during school holidays. If it was anyone but Josh I would be dead jealous, but he never brags, like some people do. Like when Marigold went to New York one time. God, we never heard the end of it! Normally he'd have called me and we'd have chatted, but after the way I'd yelled at him I felt grateful to hear from him at all.

I texted back, *Have fun Carmen xxx.* I was just so relieved that I hadn't turned him against me. Unlike Indy. I had a horrible feeling Indy might never want to speak to me again, after the way I'd treated her. Suppose she became best friends with Connie and I got squeezed out? I couldn't bear it! I knew I ought to call her and apologise. I just couldn't quite get brave enough. If only she'd had a mobile, or was on email! It would have been so much easier.

In the end I decided I would wait until half term was over. If Indy hadn't called me by then, I would *definitely* call her. And *definitely* apologise. *Definitely.*

Mum came home at six o'clock. Her eyes lit up when she saw the table all ready and laid. "Oh, how lovely! You've done it again. You're spoiling me!"

"I just took stuff out the fridge," I said.

"Yes, yes, that's fine! What's this?" She nodded at the fruit tart. "Where did that come from?"

I said, "Marks & Spencer."

"But who bought it? You bought it?"

"I thought you'd like it," I said. "It's fruit."

"It looks scrummy! But what were you doing in Marks & Spencer?"

"I went down there after school," I said. "I wanted to look in HMV." More lies. Now that I'd started, I didn't seem able to stop. "I thought you'd like something special for your tea… as a treat."

It did make me feel a bit bad when Mum gave me this big hug and said how it was a lovely thought and she really appreciated it. Mum doesn't give hugs all that often. Nan and me were always kissing and cuddling, but Mum is quite an enclosed sort of person.

"Well, it's my turn next," she said. "I'll pop out in my lunch break tomorrow and get us something really wicked… how about a raspberry pavlova?"

I said, "Wow!" She knows how I hanker after raspberry pavlovas. "All that cream and meringue?"

Mum giggled. "I know, it's shocking! Very unhealthy. But once won't hurt you… and I think you deserve it."

Needless to say, that made me feel worse than ever. But I still wasn't going back to school!

CHAPTER SIX

Next day was Saturday, which meant I was now *officially* on half term. Mum had to work, same as usual, so I thought I might as well take my guitar and go into town and do a bit more singing. After yesterday, I had got quite a taste for it. Not just for earning money; I'd still have done it even if I hadn't earned a penny, though it is good to feel that you are appreciated. It wasn't like I'd *asked* people to put anything in my doggy bowl. Nobody could accuse me of begging. They'd only done it because they thought I was worth it. I'd kept them entertained, and this was their way of thanking me, showing that they had enjoyed my performance. I think that is as much as anyone can ask.

Marigold would probably have turned up her nose and said they were all old, like being old meant they didn't count. It was true that if I'd done rock songs instead of show tunes they'd probably have clapped their hands over their ears and complained about the noise, and the lyrics, and said how it wasn't proper music, but I still had this great surging buzz of satisfaction when I saw their faces break into big beams, and they all fell silent, just sitting there listening. To *me*! I didn't even mind – well, I did a little bit. But not too much – when they opened their mouths and started trying to sing along, in their quavery voices all out of tune. I didn't care that they were old and that I wasn't singing my sort of song. I had them hooked, and that was all that mattered. They were under my spell!

It may seem a funny thing to say, but I can't ever imagine wanting to do drugs, or even drink alcohol. Why would I want to, when I can just get up and *sing*?

I thought at first, when I left home that morning, that I wouldn't go back to Sheepscombe, I'd take a different bus and go a bit further afield. After all, I didn't want to be singing the same songs all over again to the same people; I needed a change of audience. But then a number twenty came along, and that is the bus for Sheepscombe, and before I knew what I was doing I had jumped on it and stayed on it, and once I got there I couldn't really think of any place to stand except the paved area opposite M&S, where I'd stood before. I mean, there just isn't anywhere else that's suitable. With any luck, the old lady – Mrs P, as she'd said to call her – would stay indoors, snoozing in one of her pale green chairs on her dark green carpet, which was what an old lady should do. She'd been out yesterday, she didn't need to come out again. I didn't *want* her to come, bullying and bossing me and going on about straining my voice. All the same, I kept a sharp lookout, just in case.

By midday, when she hadn't put in an appearance, I told myself that I could relax; she obviously wasn't coming. That was good. That was what I wanted. I didn't *need* any bossy old person nagging at me. At the same time I had this curious feeling of having been let down, which didn't make any sense at all.

I was just deciding that I might as well pack up and go home when I saw her, tottering across from the bus station. Immediately I began on another song, one of Nan's favourites from *My Fair Lady*, but instead of belting it out, full throttle, like I normally would, I made this determined effort to hold myself back. I swooned it, and crooned it, making my voice drip like honey. Rather revolting, to my way of thinking. But I did it just to show her! I didn't *have* to be Judy Garland; I could be slow and slurpy, if that was what she wanted.

She stood listening, with her head to one side, her beady eyes fixed on my face. When I'd finished, she came up to me and said, "Dear me! What was that all about?"

I said somewhat rebelliously that I was resting my voice. "Like you told me to!"

She smiled at that, and shook her head. "How long have you been here this morning?"

"Not long." It was true, I hadn't arrived till nearly eleven.

"Quite long enough," she said, "I am sure – especially after yesterday's marathon. How would it be if I were to offer you some lunch?"

I hesitated. There was one part of me that wanted to get all haughty and on its high horse and say, "Thank you, but I am meeting my boyfriend." Then there was another part which was just dying to go back and have another look at all the photographs and posters and hear the old woman tell me again that my voice was a special gift.

"If you're worried that you haven't earned enough money…" She poked delicately at the coins in my doggy bowl with the tip of her walking stick.

"No!" I stooped, and snatched the bowl up. "I'm not doing it for the money."

"Ah! Well, that's good to know. Come, then! Let us go and eat."

Mum would really have approved of the stuff she gave us for lunch. Stuffed vine leaves, with cherry tomatoes, followed by some kind of fruit salad with all exotic kinds of fruits. Passion fruit and kiwi fruit, and some I didn't even know the name of. I bet she got it from M&S! She looked like the sort of person that would shop there.

"A light lunch, I know," she said, "but you can't sing on a full stomach."

I told her that actually I was probably going to go home. "I wasn't going to do any more today."

"Oh, not out there," she said. "I agree! But in here, for me. I thought maybe a few scales… unless, of course, you have something else planned?"

I would *so* like to have been a bit sophisticated! A bit cool and casual. *I suppose I could always stay on just a little while longer, if you really want…* Instead, I heard my voice eagerly assuring her that I had nothing whatsoever planned and would love to do some scales.

As a matter of fact, scales were quite fun. I enjoyed doing scales! What I wasn't so keen on were the breathing exercises. They were quite boring, and I didn't see why I needed them.

"I never run out of breath!"

She still insisted. She made me lie on the floor and relax, taking in great lungfuls of air and holding them, then putting my hands on my waist so that I could feel my diaphragm.

"Do you feel how it goes in and out? That's the muscle which supports your voice. It's very important it should be kept in trim. A flabby diaphragm is no good to anyone!"

She said that if I were really serious about being a

singer, I should get into the habit of doing breathing exercises "every single day". I think I must have looked at her in some kind of disbelief cos she said, "It's up to you. I know you think I'm just a bossy old harridan, but one of these days you'll thank me. Now, tell me who your favourite singers are!"

That was better. I scrambled to my feet and said eagerly that my favourite male singer was Darrin O'Shea, the lead vocalist with Urban Legend, and my favourite female singer was Topaze, who sings with Chain Reaction. She hadn't heard of either of them! She hadn't even heard of the bands.

"Oh, my dear," she said, "I'm old, I'm out of touch! In my day we didn't have rock and roll. Tell me what it is you like about these two singers."

I said, "Well... Darrin O'Shea is just, like—" The hottest thing on two legs! Only I wasn't quite brave enough to say so. "He's got this really great voice," I said. "And Topaze used to go to my school and is just absolutely amazing! If I could be like anyone, it would be her."

Some hopes! Considering she's a) black and b) beautiful and c) *slim*.

"I know it's just a dream," I said. "I know I can't ever really be like Topaze. But I might be a second Judy Garland. I wouldn't sing her sort of songs, but I think I might be the same sort of singer."

Mrs P was giving me that look, with her head to one side, her bright bird eyes blinking.

"It puzzles me," she said, "why you would aspire to be like someone else. Why should you want to be *second*? Why not be first? Why not be *you*?"

I said, "Oh, well, yes! I want to be *me*. But you have to have a role model."

"There can be people you admire," she said. "I have no quarrel with that. But never lose sight of the essential you! You have your own very special qualities, and those are what you should concentrate on."

She was such an *annoying* old person. One minute she'd be lecturing me and really getting on my nerves, the next she'd be saying something flattering, like how I had special qualities, so that I'd go all melty and forget how totally irritating she had just been.

As I left she said, "Maybe next time we'll try something a bit different… a bit of real singing. But only if you promise to do your breathing exercises!"

I muttered that tomorrow was Sunday. "I won't be around, I shouldn't think." I didn't want her to start taking things for granted. "And next week... I dunno. I dunno what I'm gonna be doing next week. I mean… I *might* be able to get in. I dunno. I can't say for certain, it all depends."

She smiled when I said that. What was there to smile about? I hadn't said anything funny. I told her that what I meant was, I couldn't make any sort of proper appointment. I know sometimes with grown-ups, and specially old ones, they like to have everything all worked out, like *when*, exactly, and *where*, exactly, and *what time*, exactly. It's no good just saying morning or afternoon, cos they get all fussed and bothered in case you might turn up when they're eating their lunch or taking a nap.

Mrs P didn't seem particularly fussed or bothered. She said, "That's all right," in soothing tones, like it was *me* getting fussed. "If you happen to be in the area, you know where to find me. I'll be here all day, I'm not going anywhere."

I asked Mum that evening if we could get some peppermint tea. She said, "Peppermint *tea*?" You'd have thought I'd asked for drain cleaner, or something. "What do you want peppermint tea for?"

"Just thought it would be nice."

"Well, it wouldn't be, it would be a sheer waste of money. You wouldn't drink it."

"I would drink it! It's good for you."

Mum said, "Oh yes? Since when have you been interested in things that are good for you?"

"I've tried it," I said. "I *like* it!"

"Might just as well drink a mug of hot water," said Mum. "Where did you try it?"

"At Indy's." I said it absolutely without hesitation. I didn't even blush. I was becoming a hardened liar! But I didn't want to tell Mum about Mrs P; she would only batter me with questions, like who was she, and where had I met her. It was just all too complicated.

Next day being Sunday I didn't really have much excuse for going anywhere. I could have said I was meeting Indy, but then suppose she went and rang while I was out? She doesn't always call me on my mobile. Mum would pick up the phone, and how embarrassing would *that* be? *Oh, I thought you were supposed to be meeting each other?*

I could say I was going to see Josh; Mum didn't know he was in Malta. Except suppose she found out? Then what would I say?

God, this was ridiculous! It was like being in a spy movie. I guess it's what happens when you start leading a double life.

Brightly, I told Mum that I was going to go into town and look round the shops. "I could buy some peppermint tea while I'm there. And I *might* go over to Indy's." Lies, lies, *lies.* "Is that OK?"

"Fine by me," said Mum. She was having her Sunday lie-in and couldn't have cared less. "Just make sure you're back by tea time – and don't expect me to drink that peppermint muck!"

There wasn't any health-food store down at Sheepscombe but I discovered that Tesco did peppermint tea, and while I was there I got two strawberry tarts for Mrs P, as I reckoned it was the sort of thing she might like. She didn't seem all that surprised when she opened the door and found me standing there. She said, "Well done! Just in time for lunch." She did seem surprised when I handed her the strawberry tarts.

"For me? Well, that is a kind thought! Very much appreciated."

She tried to get me to eat one. I was really tempted cos I adore strawberry tarts, but I know that they are probably fattening, what with the cream and the pastry, and true to her word Mum had bought a raspberry pavlova for last night's tea. I do think you have to be a *little* bit disciplined. (Unless you are like Indy, who could eat raspberry pavlovas every day for an entire month and not put on any weight.) I made the excuse to Mrs P that "You can't sing on a full stomach."

She laughed at that and said, "A lesson well learned! I, however, can eat as much as I like. My singing days are over; yours are just beginning. Did you do your breathing exercises?"

I said that I had, and this time I wasn't lying. I had actually done them before I got up! She was pleased about that. She said, "It shows you are serious. It's no good having a voice if you're not prepared to do the hard work. Let us begin!"

We started off with scales again, and then she said she wanted me to sing *Auld Lang Syne* "Very slowly and gently, as if it's a love song. Hold on to those notes… don't rush them. Slo-o-o-w, slo-o-ow... long, deep breaths… this is where your exercises will pay off."

Well! I could hold the notes, no problem, so I still didn't really see why I had to do her boring exercises, not that I dared say so. She had this habit, if she thought you were being stupid, of making her lips go all tight and thin, and sort of *shrivelling* you with her beady eyes. But I reckon she must have guessed what I was thinking cos very sharply she said, "You won't be young for ever, you know! If you really wish to make a career as a singer you need to lay the foundations *now*, before your muscles get set in their ways. Unless, of course, you're planning to retire by the time you reach thirty?"

I felt like retorting that by the time I reached thirty I'd be so old I'd be past it anyway, but I knew that would be silly, and in any case Mrs P wasn't the sort of person you talked back to. I didn't want her to shrivel me. I wanted her to… well! Be impressed. It somehow seemed important.

We worked for about an hour, and then she said that was enough for one day. "Now we'll sit down and have a little chat."

I wasn't sure I liked the sound of that. What did we have to chat about? I perched myself gingerly on the edge of the sofa and waited for her to say something. I wasn't going to say anything! It was up to her, not me.

"All right." She leaned forward. "Tell me why you aren't going in for this talent contest. What is it called? Top Pop?"

I said, "Top Spot."

"Top Spot! Why aren't you putting yourself in for it?"

I wriggled, uncomfortably. Of all the things I didn't want to talk about, this was the one I most didn't want to.

"How do your parents feel? Have you discussed it with them?"

Slowly, I shook my head.

"Why not? Aren't they interested?"

I said, "Not specially. My nan used to be." And then, before I knew it, I was telling her all about Nan and her great ambitions for me, and all about Mum, who just wished I would lose weight and not bring shame upon her, and all about the dad I'd never known, on account of Mum not actually being a hundred per cent sure who he was.

"She went to Spain," I said, "and got drunk and can't remember. It could have been a Spanish boy." I like to think of myself being half Spanish. I do have dark hair and brown eyes, whereas Mum is quite blonde, so maybe it could be true and not just a romantic fantasy. "It's why she called me Carmen," I added.

"Well, Carmen is a good name. Excellent for a singer! Imagine if you were called Daphne Bloggs – or Lily Banks, if it comes to that."

Now she was being kind, and trying to cheer me up. I'd probably got a bit self-pitying talking about Nan and Mum and my non-existent dad. I agreed that Carmen wasn't a bad sort of name, as names go. Nowhere near as lovely as Topaze, of course, though I don't suppose she was actually *christened* Topaze. On the other hand, she might have been.

Mrs P said, "Your first name's Carmen, but what is your surname?"

When I said "Bell", she clapped her hands.

"Carmen Bell! Wonderful! You see, you have an advantage over some people straight away. All right, then, Carmen Bell! Why are you not entering yourself in this talent contest?"

I might have known she wouldn't give up. I humped a shoulder and muttered, "I dunno."

"What do you mean, you don't know? With a voice like yours? That is totally absurd! I can't imagine you'd have much in the way of competition. Tell me at once what the problem is. Speak up! Don't be bashful."

I said, "I'm not bashful."

"So what is the problem?"

"Haven't got a problem."

"*Carmen Bell.*" She sat up, very stiff and straight. "Tell me the truth!"

I couldn't look at her. I had to whisper it to the carpet. "I'm too fat."

"*What?*" She leaned forward. "You're too *what?*"

I said, "Fat!"

"Too fat? Who gave you that idea? Not your mother, I hope!"

I shook my head.

"Then who?"

"Girls at school."

"*Thin* girls, I make no doubt. Do they have good voices?"

"Not specially." Marigold has a voice like a police siren. Ashlee can't even sing in tune.

"So what does it matter what they say? Surely it's the voice which counts? That plus the personality – of which, I may say, you have more than your fair share!"

I frowned. She didn't know what it was like to be sneered at and made fun of.

"Come here a moment." She stood up, and beckoned me across the room. "This is a photograph of me, at the start of my career. I wasn't exactly what you would call pretty, was I?"

I hesitated. What did she want me to say?

"Oh, come along, Carmen Bell! Be honest! I was a very *plain* young girl. Very plain. And even worse as a middle-aged woman." She moved across to another photo. "Age does not generally improve a person's looks. Alas! I always so longed to be beautiful. Or even just moderately attractive. I remember at school one year – I must have been fifteen, sixteen – they were auditioning for the end of term show. Something by Gilbert and Sullivan. I overheard two of the girls in my year discussing who was likely to get the lead. They said, 'Lily's the best singer, but she is such a *fright*.' And then they giggled – you know how girls giggle – and one of them said, 'She'd be all right for a horror film!' I was so mortified, I almost didn't audition. But then I thought, *I'm not going to let two silly girls get the better of me!* So I went ahead, and I got the part, and I never looked back. I'm not saying it's easy, but you have to have faith in yourself."

She broke off, to study me. "You're not convinced!

What makes you think that plain Lily Banks might have been able to do it, but not Carmen Bell?"

"You sang in opera!" It burst out of me before I could stop it. "Opera's different. Nobody cares what people in opera look like!"

"Oh, my dear, that is where you are so wrong. People always care what you look like. *Always*. Maybe they shouldn't – but they do. You have to learn to make the best of yourself. Dress well, move well, speak well… me, I knew I could never be beautiful, but at least I could be smart." She waved a hand at the photograph. "After a bit, people stopped thinking how plain I was and thought how elegant I was. Now, you—" She cupped my chin in her hand, forcing me to look up at her. "You have so much! You have a face I would have died for. Skin I would have died for. *Hair* I would have died for! I always had to wear a hair piece. I would have looked at you with such envy! And on top of all this, you have a voice which is pure gold. Don't, I beg you, let any stupid girls prevent you from using it!"

I don't know why it is, but I get the prickles all over when people pay me compliments. I just can't take it! Anyone says anything nice to me and I go into some kind of mad, squirming overdrive. Sternly, I turned to the photograph she'd been pointing to.

"That thing round your neck," I said. "Is it *fur*?"

"I'm afraid it is." She gave a little laugh. Sort of apologetic, but not terribly. "We weren't very enlightened in those days."

"Go out in it now," I said, "you'd probably get paint chucked over you."

"Is that what you would like to do? Chuck paint over it? Well, it's still in my wardrobe, I can fetch it for you, if you like. I don't have any paint, but I have some red nail polish, if that would do."

I scowled, and moved away. "'S all right. 'S not gonna save the animal, is it?"

Gravely she said, "No – but it's not too late to save *you*. Please! Don't give up so easily. Don't let those foolish girls get the better of you."

Nag, nag, nag! Why couldn't she just mind her own business?

"Don't you feel the urge to get up there and show them? Have you no fighting spirit? I'm sure, if your nan were here, she'd back me up."

Angrily, I said, "My nan wouldn't ever try to make me do something I didn't want to do! She was on *my* side."

"And so am I, my dear, believe it or not."

"Well, don't be!" I yelled. "I don't want you on my side! Just leave me alone!"

I felt bad afterwards. But she shouldn't have brought Nan into it! She had no right. Nan always loved me and stuck up for me. She'd have given Mrs P a right ear bashing. I could just hear her. *You let that girl be! She'll make her own mind up what she wants to do. She doesn't need the likes of you shoving your oar in.*

Oh, I did miss Nan! I missed her *so much*. More and more as the weeks went by. I didn't have anyone now; I'd even managed to upset both of my two best friends.

All I had left was this horrible old woman, who nagged me.

That night when I went to bed I called Indy. If she'd answered the phone, I would have apologised to her. I would have made things right between us! But nobody came; there wasn't even any message service. Just the ringing of the phone in the empty flat. It seemed like even Indy had gone away for half term. Either that, or she was out for the day. I knew she had an auntie who lived near London, and cousins she used to play with. I pictured her there with them, laughing and happy and not ever once thinking of me, cos why should she? I'd yelled at her. Told her I wouldn't ever speak to her again.

I just felt so *alone*.

CHAPTER SEVEN

I didn't go out at all either on Monday or on Tuesday, just stayed in and moped. I couldn't settle to anything. I tried a bit of telly, but it was all so rubbish I had to switch it off. Then I tried a bit of reading, a book we'd been doing in class. I thought maybe I should catch up on what I'd missed, but then I thought what was the point? The book was dead boring anyway. Everything was boring. I couldn't even listen to my music – she'd even gone and ruined that for me. It didn't matter how high I turned the volume up, I still kept hearing her tinny old voice nagging at me. I began to wish I'd never met her. I wanted Josh! I wanted Indy! I wanted everything to be *normal.*

If things had been normal, I'd probably have been meeting Indy in the shopping centre. We'd have wandered round, looking at stuff, pointing out any boys we happened to fancy, having a bit of a giggle. Or maybe I'd have caught the bus and gone round her place and we'd have listened to CDs and played with her little brother. Nothing special. We never really did anything special; we didn't need to. We were just happy being together.

I kept wondering whether Indy was home yet, and if so what she was doing. I tortured myself, imagining her wandering round the shopping centre with Connie instead of me. Imagining *Connie* going back to her place, playing with Darren. I loved that little boy! He'd once told me I was his favourite girl friend. I couldn't bear the thought of Connie taking my place.

I knew I ought to try ringing again. It was up to me to make the first move, not Indy. I actually picked up the phone, several times, and started punching out numbers. But when it came to the point, I got, like, paralysed and couldn't go through with it. Truth to tell, I was scared. Me and Indy had never quarrelled before, and I didn't know how to handle the situation. Suppose I rang and she said, "I don't want to talk to you any more," and slammed the phone down? Even just the thought of it shrivelled me.

When Mum arrived home on Tuesday she was considerably annoyed that I hadn't done anything. Hadn't washed up, hadn't got dinner, hadn't even bothered getting dressed.

"For goodness sake, Carmen! What have you been up to all day? Go and put some clothes on. You look like a slattern!"

Whatever that may be. I slouched off angrily into my bedroom and yanked on a sack-like T-shirt and a pair of baggy jeans. Mum pursed her lips, but didn't actually say anything. Just as well, or I might have exploded. I'd been nagged quite enough by Mrs P, I didn't need Mum having a go at me as well.

Next morning she came into my room – where I was still attempting to *sleep* – and said, "I don't know why you were in such a bad temper last night, but I don't want to come home to the same thing this evening. What are you doing all day? What have you got planned?"

I mumbled that I didn't have anything planned. Mum said, "Why don't you go and visit someone?"

Like who?

"There must be somebody," said Mum. "What's happened to all your friends?"

I snapped, "Nothing's happened to them! They've gone on holiday. People do," I said. "*Normal* people."

"Don't you get on my case," said Mum. "What's put

you in such a foul mood? Maybe you'd better come to the salon and I'll see if I can fit you in for a facial."

That got me shooting up the bed. "It's all right," I said. "I'm going out."

I hated visiting Mum at the salon. Everyone there was stick thin and gorgeous, and I always felt that before I arrived Mum was probably apologising in advance for having a daughter that couldn't squeeze into a size six. I knew she was secretly ashamed of me.

"I've just remembered… I've got things to do."

"What things?" said Mum.

"I dunno! Just things. Like… *things*."

"Well, make sure you have your phone with you. I like to know that I can reach you."

I *could* have taken a chance and gone to Indy's. Or I could have been brave and called first, to make sure she was there and that she was still talking to me. But I didn't do either. Instead, I caught the number twenty bus and went to Sheepscombe. If I'd taken my guitar I could have pretended I was going there to sing, but I left the guitar where it was, in my bedroom. I knew I wasn't going to sing – well, not to my adoring public. (OK, I'm only joking! Though one old man did actually call out to me as I walked across the square: "No songs today?")

I'm not sure what I'd have done if Mrs P had been out. She was way the most provoking old person I'd ever met, but at least when I was with her I felt alive and tingling with energy. After two days just mooching about at home, I felt like some kind of slug.

I was relieved when she opened the door but a bit embarrassed, as well, considering how I'd flounced out on Sunday. It never really occurred to me, though, that she might not want to see me any more. I find that odd, as I don't think I'd have wanted to see me; I had been kind of unpleasant. I think I might have shut the door in my face. Mrs P just very calmly nodded and said, "So there you are. The prima donna returns. I wondered if you'd have the pluck."

I started stammering out excuses, but she waved a hand, a bit impatiently, and said, "Never mind all that!

Come in, come in, don't just stand there. I presume you've come to do some work?"

She kept me at it all morning, and I really enjoyed it. We did scales and exercises and she said I had a very good range. I glowed at that! Fortunately she didn't ask me if I'd done my breathing exercises. I wouldn't have liked to lie to her, but I'm not sure I'd have been bold enough to admit that I hadn't. I just hated it when she gave me one of those beady-eyed looks of hers, like I was totally beneath contempt and not worth bothering with.

At the end of two hours she said that that was probably enough. "We should have some lunch now, and then I must send you on your way."

I said, "It's all right, I don't have to be back till tea time." I could have gone on all afternoon! "We can do some more exercises, if you like, I'm not in the least bit tired."

She said, "No, my dear, I'm sure you're not. But I'm an old lady, and old ladies need their rest."

I hadn't thought about that. Of course I knew she *was* an old lady, far older even than Nan had been, but when she was at the piano, barking out her orders – "Gently, gently! You're not selling potatoes!" – I tended to forget how ancient she was.

"Can I come again tomorrow?" I said.

"On one condition." She did the beady-eyed thing, but not like I was beneath contempt, more like she was about to issue some kind of challenge. "You must sing a song for me. Not" – she held up a hand – "not just any old song. The song you would sing if you were going in for the contest."

She was doing it again! *Nagging* at me.

"I'm sure you must have thought about it. You must have a favourite song."

I could feel my face scrunching itself up into a scowl.

"Oh, now, come along, come along!" she said. "I'm no threat, I'm just an old woman. What would you sing?"

Sullenly, I muttered, "Something I wrote with a friend."

"Splendid! Then please, tomorrow, come prepared to sing it for me."

"You wouldn't like it," I said. "It's not your sort of music."

Her pencilled eyebrows rose in a sort of cool disdain, like I'd said something really stupid. "Music is music," she said. "There are only two sorts – good music and bad music. If you think your song is bad music, then fair enough. Don't sing it! Do you think it's bad music?"

I wriggled, uncomfortably. "It's rock."

"Yes?" She stood, waiting.

"It's sort of… loud."

"So I would suppose. In my experience, rock usually is."

"But you've just been telling me to sing *quietly*!"

"My dear, that was an exercise! What I'm asking for is a performance. Are you going to sing it for me, or not?"

I shrugged. "Could. I s'pose."

"I shall expect it. Tomorrow morning, eleven o'clock. Please be punctual. *And don't forget those breathing exercises!*"

I spent all that evening in my room, practising *Star Crazy Me*. Mum banged on the door at one point and told me to "Stop making so much noise, for goodness sake!" but I just stuffed pillows at the bottom of the door and carried on. If I was going to sing for Mrs P, then it had to be as good as I could possibly make it. I don't know whether the pillows actually did anything to muffle the sound, but Mum didn't come yelling at me again. Maybe she just shut the sitting-room door and turned the telly up.

Next morning, after Mum had gone to work, I did my breathing exercises. I had this feeling Mrs P had known, yesterday, that I hadn't been doing them. Maybe not actually *known*, but she'd definitely suspected. I didn't want her asking me and me having to lie. Somehow, telling Mrs P I'd done her exercises when I hadn't seemed even worse than the really *whopping* great lie I'd told Mum about being in school when I'd spent the day wandering round the shopping centre. Not that I would expect Mum to agree with me; she would certainly go ballistic if she ever found out. But I could cope with Mum's rage. What I couldn't face was the thought of Mrs P's contempt. It just shrivelled me!

She'd said to go round at eleven o'clock. I was so anxious not to be late that I arrived half an hour early and had to kill time looking at clothes in Marks & Spencer. I knew if she'd said eleven, she meant eleven, and not quarter to or quarter past. She was that sort of person. I'd brought my guitar with me so I suppose I could have done a bit of singing, but I wanted to preserve my voice for later. I'd never have thought of such a thing before. Preserving my voice! That was Mrs P's influence, that was.

I rang her doorbell at *exactly* eleven o'clock. She seemed pleased. She said, "Good girl! On the dot. And

I see you've come prepared." She nodded at my guitar. "Excellent!"

We had such a good morning. We did the usual scales and exercises, and she got me singing a few songs, such as *Amazing Grace*, for breath control and vowel sounds, and said she was "very happy" with the way things were going.

"It's a pleasure working with you! Now, let us break for a bite of lunch, then you shall sing me your song."

And that was where it all started to go pear-shaped. Not the actual song. I gave it all I'd got...

Star crazy me
Floatin' free-ee-ee
Into the ether of
Eternity...

I did all five verses. I was really flying! I knew, whatever she said, it wasn't her kind of music, but I was up there, on stage, in the spotlight, with everybody going wild. I almost half expected, at the end, to hear applause. Thunderous applause! What I didn't expect was silence.

Defensively I said, "I told you you wouldn't like it."

"Oh, my dear, quite the contrary," she said. "I am impressed! I asked for a performance, you gave me a performance. To sing like that, for an audience of just one old woman, is no mean achievement. And didn't it make you feel good? Didn't it make you just long to get up and sing in front of a *real* audience?"

She was doing it again! She was going to start nagging.

"Well?" She gave me the beady eye. "*Didn't* it?"

Why did she always, *always* have to go and ruin everything? It had been so lovely up until then! Resentfully I said, "I've sung in front of a real audience. You've heard me sing in front of a real audience!"

"Oh!" She waved a hand. "The denizens!"

I wasn't sure what denizens were, exactly, but if she meant the old people, then I thought it was extremely rude and ageist of her. I mean, what did she think *she* was?

"It's still singing," I said.

"Oh, to be sure! Show tunes for the grannies! All very sweet, and you sang them very well, but it's not where your heart is, is it? Follow your dreams, my dear! *Go for it*, I believe, is the modern expression. Be brave! Confound the lot of them! Sing your song and prove what you can do."

How many times did I have to tell her? *I was not going in for that talent contest.*

"Well?" She barked it at me. "Cat got your tongue?"

I stood there, tugging at a bit of broken fingernail, and all the time feeling her beady gaze fixed on me.

"I can see we are not going to get anywhere. That being the case" – she moved across to the piano and began briskly stacking sheets of music – "it is obviously time to take action. Broaden your horizons. Tomorrow I am going to the opera. I had intended going with a friend, but she has had to back out. That means I have a spare ticket. I think perhaps you had better come with me."

To the *opera*? She had to be kidding!

"Don't worry, it's nothing frightening. As a matter of fact, it's *your* opera – *Carmen.* Very tuneful! Up in town, so we wouldn't be back until late... eleven, eleven fifteen. But that's all right – I'll send you home in a cab, or you can stay the night here, whichever you prefer."

In a weird sort of way – I mean, considering I didn't like opera – it was actually quite tempting. The thought of going up to town, to a real theatre. A posh one, probably, if it was opera. Then coming back late and getting cabs... that was what rich people did! But how could I explain to Mum? I couldn't! I'd have to tell so many lies. It would just get too complicated.

"What's the matter?" She turned to look at me. "Cat actually bitten your tongue right out?"

I pulled a face. The childish sort of face you pull in

Reception when a teacher tells you you've been naughty. I said, "What would I want to go and see an opera for?"

"Well..." She smiled sweetly at me. "Since you manifestly don't have enough backbone to pursue your real ambition, you should maybe cast your net a bit wider and try something different... find something new to aim for. A new ambition!"

"I don't want a new ambition!"

"So what do you actually intend to do with your life?"

"Not sing in opera!"

"No..." She nodded, slowly. "Upon reflection, you are probably right. I doubt you'd get very far in that world, either. It's a cut-throat business – you have to be prepared to take a lot of knocks. It probably wouldn't suit you."

"I don't want it to suit me! I don't want to be an *opera* singer."

"No, you don't," she said, "you want to be a rock

star. You have the voice to be a rock star. You have the voice, you have the talent – all you lack is the determination. How was it your song went? *This crazy gal will reach the top?* I'm sorry, but I don't think so! Not with that attitude. It seems a shame to waste the gifts you've been given, but unless you're prepared to stand up and fight you might as well stop dreaming right here and now and admit that you're going to end up as just another nobody."

Furiously, I retorted, "There's nothing wrong with being a nobody!"

"You're right, there isn't – if you have no other ambition. But I think you have! Haven't you? Oh, now, for heaven's sake, if you're going to sulk you'd better go. Go home and think about things. You can come and see me again tomorrow, but only if you feel like talking."

I snarled, "I *can't* come tomorrow, I'm *doing* things!"

"Well, whenever you've had a chance to stiffen that backbone… you know where to find me."

I went off in a huff, banging the front door as I did so. Arrogant, ugly old bag! Telling me I hadn't any backbone! I had backbone. I could stand up for myself! I'd told Marigold Johnson a thing or two. How dare she? How *dare* she?

I hurtled down the steps and out into the square so blinded with rage that I went barging straight into someone walking past. As we bounced off each other, I realised it was Stacey Kingsley, from my class at school. She seemed as surprised to see me as I was to see her. She said, "What're you doing here?"

I said, "What're you?"

She told me she had come to visit her nan.

I said, "What, she lives in the flats?"

"Nah!" She shook her head. "She's in the old people's home. D'you actually know someone who lives in this block?"

"My singing teacher," I said.

"Your *singing* teacher?"

"Mrs P. That's what I call her. She used to be

famous in opera. She's got this huge flat – that one there." I pointed. "It's all full of precious antiques and stuff."

"Wow." I could tell Stacey was impressed. So she should be! "You gotta be rolling in it to live there."

"Yes, she's stinking rich," I said.

"And she teaches you singing?"

"Every day, she gives me these lessons. She's taking me to the opera tomorrow. *Carmen.* That's my opera." I couldn't resist a bit of boasting. "What my mum called me after."

"You're called after an *opera*?"

"Yup. Spanish, cos that's what my dad was."

"D'you *like* opera?"

"'S all right. The best bit's going up to town. We'll probably have a meal somewhere, some posh restaurant, cos we're going to be really late back... eleven o'clock, maybe later. She'll get a cab to take me home. Cab's nothing to her."

Stacey said, "We got a cab all the way to the airport one time."

"Yeah?"

"Yeah."

"Mrs P gets them all over the place."

"Is she old?" said Stacey.

"Pretty ancient. She's got pots of money, though. She was a really big star, way back."

"So how d'you get to meet her?"

I was about to say that she'd heard me singing, but then it suddenly struck me: Stacey's nan could have been one of the old people who'd put money in my doggy bowl. I wouldn't want Stacey finding out about that.

I said, "I didn't exactly meet her, I—" And then I glanced at my watch and gave an exaggerated yelp. "Omigod, look at the time! I gotta go!"

"OK," said Stacey. "See ya."

"Yeah!" I galloped off across the square. "See ya!"

It wasn't until I went to bed that night that I realised: I had left my guitar behind…

CHAPTER EIGHT

I couldn't have gone round to Mrs P's next day even if I'd wanted, which I didn't, except that some time I was going to have to face her, just to get my guitar back. But Friday was Mum's day off, and she'd already made arrangements for us to go and visit my Auntie Angela. She insisted that I had to go with her.

"We hardly ever do anything together! Of course you have to come."

Mum could never understand why I didn't want to, and there wasn't any way I could explain to her. Auntie Anje is Mum's sister; she's slim and gorgeous-looking, just like Mum. She has two daughters called Tiffany and Bethan, and they are slim and gorgeous-looking, too. I would like to be able to say that they are also mean and vain and spiteful, but in fact they are none of those things. They are quite good-natured and friendly, which just makes it all the worse as it means I have no excuse for not wanting to see them. It's entirely my own fault if I always end up feeling totally inadequate and dissatisfied with myself. No one ever *says* that compared to Tiffy and Beth I am gross and fat and lumpy. No one even hints at it; they are too kind. But I know that is what they are thinking, and I know that Mum is envious of Auntie Anje for having produced two such teensy tiny delicate little creatures while all she has got for her trouble is a great sack of lard.

Auntie Anje said she was pleased we'd come over as Tiffy wanted to ask Mum something. She wanted to know, next year when she had work experience, whether she could do it in Mum's salon.

"I really, really, *really* want to be a beautician!"

Mum, needless to say, was delighted. I could see that for her it would be an opportunity to do a little bit of showing off, for a change. She might have a great ungainly lump of a daughter, but at least she could lay claim to a beautiful niece. I didn't blame Mum, not one little bit, but it's no use pretending that it didn't hurt, cos it did.

Bethan piped up to say that *she* was going to be an air hostess. Mum cried, "Yes! You certainly have the looks for it."

I didn't know air hostesses needed looks, but I guess it's something to distract the passengers and stop them thinking about crash landings and hijackers. They are really just waitresses, though; I wouldn't want to be one. When Auntie Anje turned to me and asked, "What about you, Carmen? What are you planning to do?" the words came bursting out of my mouth before I could stop them: "I certainly wouldn't want to be an air hostess!"

There was then a long, awkward silence, which Mum finally broke by pointing out they weren't called air hostesses, these days. "They're flight attendants."

I could see everyone thinking, *Yes, and they don't have fat ones.* This is what I mean about it being my own fault. Auntie Anje did her best to patch things up. She said, "What about your singing? Nan did so love it! She used to tell everyone about her granddaughter… going to be a second Judy Garland."

I said, "That was when I was young and didn't know any better."

"Any better than what?" said Mum.

"Being a second Judy Garland. I don't want to be a second *anybody*! I want to be me."

"Well, hoity toity!" said Mum. "There's gratitude for you! Your poor old nan thought she was paying you a compliment."

"She was always so proud of you," said Auntie Anje. "It used to make my two quite jealous, didn't it, girls?"

They nodded solemnly.

"Anyway" – Mum said it in the no-nonsense voice she uses when she reckons I'm getting above myself – "being you isn't exactly what I'd call a career move. You'll need to think of something a bit more practical than that!"

I was glad when at last we could go home. I felt so angry with myself! I always swore that *this time* I would be cool, I would be sophisticated, I wouldn't let feelings of inferiority push me into making sour and bitter remarks. When would I ever learn???

Next day was Saturday and Mum had to work, so I decided I would go and get my guitar back. I would be polite, but firm.

"I am sorry to bother you, but I have just come to pick up my guitar."

No scales, no exercises. *No talking.* Just the guitar. If she happened to invite me in – well! I might accept, I might not. It would depend how she asked me. If she was in one of her barking moods, I'd say thank you, but I had somewhere to go. If, on the other hand, she looked like she was prepared to be pleasant and not start nagging at me, then maybe I would go in for just half an hour. Just to be polite. It was up to her.

There wasn't any reply when I rang at her doorbell. I rang and rang, in case she'd fallen asleep like Nan used to, but nobody came. I felt a bit cross. I'd made all this effort, and now she wasn't there! She ought to be there. It was still only ten o'clock and she'd been out late last night. Maybe she was still in bed and too deaf to hear the bell?

I was about to hammer at the door with my fist when an old lady appeared, tottering down the hall. "If you're looking for Mrs P," she said, "she's in the hospital."

I said, "Oh no!" It's terrible, but my first thought – well, maybe my second –was for my guitar. How was I going to get it back???

"Taken there last night," said the old lady. "Mugged, she was. Some young thug in a hood, waiting for her as she came in. Smashed the light, didn't they? I always told her, you're asking for trouble, coming home that time of night. It's just not safe. Not these days."

Disturbing thoughts started to whiz round my head. "Is she going to be all right?" I whispered.

"Who knows? She's no spring chicken… eighty-five last birthday. You don't bounce back so fast at that age. I'll be going to visit her later on. Can I give her a message?"

I couldn't think of anything suitable. My mind was heaving and churning.

"Shall I tell her you called? What name shall I say?"

"C-Carmen. Did they rob her?"

"Took her lovely rings that she wears, and her jewellery. And her bag, of course. Fortunately Mr Dyer from upstairs heard the rumpus and came down to investigate, or they'd have been inside, helping themselves."

"I s'pose they didn't catch anyone?"

"Not a chance! Soon as Mr Dyer appeared, the young so-and-so made off. Ought to be strung up, if you ask me, attacking an old lady like that. Anyway, I'll tell her you were here."

I wandered back in a daze across the square. What was I supposed to do now? My guitar was locked up in Mrs P's flat and Mrs P was in hospital and might not come out, and I was beginning to be horribly scared that I might have been responsible for putting her there. Me and my stupid boasting! Stacey Kingsley wasn't one of Marigold's particular friends but she did go round with Craig Archer, and Craig Archer just happened to be Lance Stapleton's best buddy, and everyone knew Lance Stapleton was a thug. He was exactly the type that would hang around in doorways waiting for old ladies to mug. If Stacey had told Craig about me and Mrs P going to the opera and not getting back till eleven o'clock, Craig could easily have given Lance a tip-off.

It wasn't like Craig himself was any angel; *he'd* had run-ins with the cops before now, though only for minor things. I didn't think he'd actually resort to bodily harm. But Lance would! He was known for it. He wouldn't think anything of attacking an old lady.

I began to feel a bit desperate. Mrs P had been good to me, and I'd been nothing but rude and ungracious. It was true she'd nagged me and bullied me and told me I didn't have any backbone, but even while I was getting mad at her I think I'd known, really, that she wasn't doing it to upset me. She was doing it because she believed in me. She really believed that I had a voice! And all I'd done in return was sulk. And now I'd probably gone and got her mugged, and if she died it would be my fault.

I blundered on, back to the bus stop. I kept picturing Mrs P, dressed in her finery, all happy after seeing her beloved opera, never suspecting that some horrible thug was waiting for her in the shadows. I couldn't bear the thought of her being beaten up! She was such a frail old lady.

While I was waiting at the bus stop, wondering what to do, I got a text message. From Josh! All it said was, *Hi U.* I immediately texted back, asking where he was. He said he was home. *Where U?* I said that I was in Sheepscombe. Josh said, *Doing what?* I said, *Nothing.*

Next thing I know, he's actually calling me. We're actually speaking!

Josh said, "Wanna come over?"

I told him, *Yes.* Yes, yes, yes! I said that I would come straight away.

Josh said, "Good, cos I've got something to tell you."

I said, "What?" But he said not over the phone.

I felt a bit apprehensive. I said, "Is it something nice?"

"Dunno 'bout nice."

"It's not anything *nasty*?"

"No, it's not anything nasty! Just get over here."

I couldn't wait to see Josh again. I did so want things to be back the way they'd always been! I'd felt so isolated, without either him or Indy. You really do need your friends, I think; it's miserable, being on your own.

I did have one moment of panic as I got to Josh's place, thinking maybe we wouldn't have anything to say to each other, but I needn't have worried. Josh was so eager to give me his news that we didn't have time for awkward pauses.

"Just thought you'd like to know," he said, "that I finally did it."

Bemused, I said, "Did what?"

"What you told me to do. What you said I was too cowardly to do!"

"You mean… you told them? Your mum and dad?"

He nodded, grinning. Obviously pleased with himself.

"What did they say?"

"Oh… you know! All the usual mum and dad type stuff."

I said, "Like what?" but he seemed reluctant to go into details so I thought probably it embarrassed him. I guessed it would have been slurpy stuff along the lines of *You're still our son* and *We'll always love you*. Stuff like out of a movie. *Exactly* what I'd predicted!

"So they didn't chuck you out?" I said.

He grinned again, and shook his head. "They were pretty relaxed about it."

"Surprise, surprise!"

"Go on, you can say it."

"Say what?"

"I told you so."

"Well, I did! It was obvious. You didn't seriously think they'd disown you?"

"No, but I knew they'd be a bit upset."

"*Are* they?"

Josh said they had to be. He said normal parents always wanted their kids to get married and have kids of their own. "They all want to be grannies and grandpas."

I said, "Really? I don't reckon my mum'd fancy that idea."

"How is your mum?" said Josh. "What did she say about you not going in to school?"

I told him that Mum didn't know. Then quickly, before he could get started, I said, "So how was Malta?"

Josh said, "Hot. How was Sheepscombe?"

"Sheeps— oh! Yes." I smiled brightly. "Hub of the universe! Same as always."

"So what were you doing there?"

"Oh, just—" I waved a hand. "I went to visit someone. This old lady." And that was when I told him about Mrs P. How I had been busking, and she had invited me back for peppermint tea. How once upon a time she'd been an opera singer – "She was *famous*!" How she'd been giving me singing lessons for free. How she'd invited me to go to the opera with her, and how I'd been so rude and unpleasant.

Josh said, "Why? Why were you rude and unpleasant?"

"I don't know!" I wasn't about to admit that it was because she kept nagging at me, and telling me I had no backbone. "I just was! But it's awful cos she went on her own and when she got back it was late and someone was waiting for her and they mugged her and stole all her lovely jewellery, and now she's in hospital and... I think it might be my fault!"

"What, just because you didn't go with her?"

"No! It's worse than that."

I told him how I'd bumped into Stacey, and how I'd boasted about all the wonderful things Mrs P had in her flat. "And then I said we were going up to town on Friday evening and wouldn't be back till really late, and you know Stacey goes round with Craig Archer, and Craig goes round with Lance Stapleton, and—"

"You think Lance did it?"

"He could have. It's exactly the sort of thing he does!"

Josh sat there, frowning. I silently begged him to tell me I was talking nonsense, but he didn't. He nodded, slowly, and said, "I guess it's possible."

"So what should I do?" The question came wailing out of me. "D'you think I should go to the police?"

"I dunno." Josh screwed up his face, considering the matter. "Maybe you should go and talk to the old lady first?"

I looked at him, doubtfully. "She's in hospital. I don't know whether she'd want to see me."

"You could give it a go."

"But I don't know which hospital she's in!"

"You could *ask*?" said Josh. "Or is that too simple?"

I sighed. "No, I s'pose not."

"It seems pretty simple to me."

"*All right!* I'll ask. Don't keep on! What have you done to your eye?" I'd noticed earlier that it was all brown and yellow, like it had been bruised. "Did you bump into something?"

"Yeah, somebody's fist."

"You're joking!"

"I'm not joking."

"You had a *fight?*" Josh isn't the sort of person to get into fights. "Who with?"

"Lance, if you must know."

Him again. I said, "That thug! He should be locked up. What happened?"

"Nothing much. I just objected to something he said."

"Why? What did he say?"

There was a silence.

"Josh!" I screamed it at him. "*What did he say?*"

"Something stupid."

"*What?*"

"I'm not going to tell you, so there's no point yelling. Just forget about it, OK? It's all over and done with."

Sometimes you have to accept when you are beaten. When Josh clams up, there's no getting anything from him. He can be *really* obstinate.

I said, "OK! But I bet I'll find out."

"Dunno how," said Josh. "That'd mean coming back

to school… You gonna come back to school?"

Crossly I said, "Might've known you'd start on that."

"I'm entitled," said Josh.

"Just cos you came out to your mum and dad!"

"That's right. Can't accuse *me* of being a coward! Not now. You're the only cowardly one!"

We stood there: me bristling, Josh triumphant. Josh said, "*Well?*"

I wasn't going to quarrel with him again. I'd *hated* the last ten days, without Josh and Indy.

"Tell me what Lance Stapleton said, then maybe…"

"What?"

"Maybe I'll think about things."

"Not good enough!"

"Why won't you tell me?"

"Why won't you go in for the contest?"

We were going round in circles. It was quite a relief when the door opened and Josh's mum came in.

"Sorry to break things up," she said, "but Josh, it

really is time we left. I promised Nan we'd be there for lunch."

His other nan, that was. Imagine having *two* nans, who both loved you! Mrs Daniels told me to jump in the car and she'd give me a lift up the road. As I got out at the entrance to our block, Josh stuck his head out the window and hissed, "*Saved by the bell!*"

There was nothing I could say in return, not in front of his mum. I had to content myself with a rude gesture and hope she didn't notice. Josh yelled, "See you Monday!" Then he closed the window back up and the car sped off down the road.

CHAPTER NINE

After Josh and his mum had gone I stood there on the pavement, wondering what to do. I couldn't go back indoors, I felt too unsettled. The inside of my head was churning. First I thought of Mrs P, then of Lance Stapleton. Then of my guitar – would I ever get it back? Then of school – what was I going to do? Then of Josh and his black eye. What could Lance have said to him? Called him names, was my bet. Something horrible. Something anti-gay. But why wouldn't he tell me?

He'd said if I wanted to find out I would have to go back to school. That meant that other people had been there when it happened; there were other people who knew. Indy, for instance. Indy would know! But was I brave enough to call her? I flipped open my mobile. *Do it! Don't think, just DO it.*

OK! I would. I hooked my hair back over my ears, like clearing the decks kind of thing. *Getting prepared.* Then I took a breath... and did it!

It was Indy's mum who answered. She said, "Hallo, stranger! Haven't heard from you for a while." At least her mum sounded friendly. Maybe Indy hadn't told her.

I swallowed and said, "Is Indy there?"

Her mum said she was. "I'll get her. *InDEEEEE!* It's Carmen."

I'd gone all tense. What would I do if she refused to

speak to me? And then I heard her voice, a bit guarded, at the other end of the line. "Carm?"

I said, "Indy?"

There was a pause. I knew that it was up to me. I opened my mouth and the words came babbling out.

"Indy I'm sorry I yelled at you I didn't mean it, it was just I was so worried about Josh in case he thought I'd given him away cos it was like this huge big secret just between the two of us and—"

"It's OK," said Indy. "I understand."

"I've kept meaning to ring you!"

"Me, too."

"I wish you had!"

"Wish you had."

Shamefaced, I mumbled, "I thought you mightn't want to hear from me any more."

"I thought you mightn't want to hear from me."

"I was just in a panic. I didn't mean it! Honest!"

There was another pause, then Indy said, "So how you doing?"

"OK. How you?"

"OK."

"You been away?"

"Went to visit my auntie. What you been up to?"

"Nothing much. Just – you know! Messing around. Listen, can I come over?"

"What, like now?" said Indy.

"I need to talk to you!"

She hesitated. "See, it's difficult," she said. She sounded a bit embarrassed. "I'm meeting Arvid."

"Arvid? You're actually going out with him?" Arvid was this boy from Year 9. I knew she fancied him, but the last I'd heard she was still at the stage of plucking up her courage to actually say something. "Did he ask you?"

"No," said Indy. "I asked him!"

"You didn't?" I couldn't believe it! Timid Indy, asking a boy to go out with her? "Tell me you're joking!"

"I'm not. He kept smiling at me like he really wanted to say something, so in the end we got talking, and—"

"How?" I said. "How did you get talking?"

"Well, you know... I said hi, and he said hi, and then we sort of... went on from there."

"And you actually asked him out?"

"I s'pose it was more like we asked each other out. If you know what I mean."

I wasn't sure that I did. I wondered how I felt about it. I stayed off school for just a few days and my best mate went and got herself a boyfriend... I'd pictured her with Connie, but I'd never even considered Arvid. I said, "So where are you meeting him?"

"Outside Gap."

"What time?"

"Two o'clock... I could always get there a bit earlier, if you like."

I grabbed eagerly at the suggestion. We arranged to meet up in twenty minutes, so I immediately went whizzing off to the bus stop to catch a bus into town.

Indy was there waiting for me on a bench.

"So what's happening?" she said. "Are you coming back to school?"

I said, "No! Yes – maybe. I don't know. I've just been to see Josh. It's awful. Everyone I know is getting beaten up!"

"Why? Who else has?" said Indy.

"This old woman that I've been seeing. She's just been mugged and it might be my fault!"

So then it all burst out of me, all over again, and I told Indy, just like I had told Josh, all about Mrs P and how she'd invited me to the opera and I'd said no *thank you*, in a rather rude sort of way.

"I'd have said the same," said Indy. "I mean, who'd want to sit through an opera?"

I said, "Nobody that had any sense, but I didn't have to be nasty about it." I didn't add that the only reason I'd been so unpleasant was that Mrs P had kept nagging me about the talent contest. I didn't want Indy starting up. "At least with Josh I don't have to feel guilty," I said. "At least *that* wasn't my fault."

"No. I s'pose not."

I looked at Indy rather sharply. Did I detect a note of doubt in her voice?

"I mean, it was Lance Stapleton, right?"

"Mm." She nodded.

"What did he say? Was he being anti-gay?"

"Ye-e-es… but that wasn't how it started."

"So how did it start?"

That was when she told me. It was Marigold again. Loud mouthing. Saying how my name was still on the list of entrants for the contest, but that I obviously wouldn't have the guts to actually go through with it.

"I mean—" Indy waved a hand. "What with her precious sister, and all."

What with me being so fat, and all. That was what she meant, only being Indy she was too kind to say it.

"What exactly happened?" I said.

"Well, Josh started laying into her. Told her she was totally mindless. Said she was a body fascist."

"Josh said that?"

"Yes, and lots of people agreed with him. So then Lance told Josh that Marigold was his girl and Josh had just better watch what he was saying, and then he called him a poof, and—"

"Then he hit him."

Indy said, "No, Josh hit *him.*"

"Josh hit *Lance*?"

"Yes, and everybody cheered! So then Lance got really mad and hit him back, and next thing we know Mr Cotton's arrived and they're being put on report."

"Both of them? That's not fair!"

"Josh did hit him first," said Indy.

"But he gave Josh a black eye!"

Indy giggled. "You should see Lance – he's all blubber-lipped! I think one of his teeth got broken."

"Wow!" I couldn't help feeling pleased, even though I strongly disapprove of violence. I think that boys punching each other is truly pathetic. Like boxing. It is just *so* barbaric. But I still felt pleased!

"So what you gonna do 'bout the old woman?" said Indy.

I sighed. "Guess I'll have to go and see her."

"Seems only right."

I knew that it was – and not just because I felt guilty. Because I owed it to her. And because I really cared. I'd sort of grown fond of her, in an odd kind of way.

"Look, there's Arvid," I said. "I'd better be going."

"You don't have to," said Indy; but I knew she wouldn't want me hanging around. Not on her first date.

I told her to have fun, and quickly made myself scarce. I still didn't feel like going home. I felt like it even less now than I had before. The thought of Josh going off to see his nan, and Indy going off with her new boyfriend, made me all tearful and self-pitying. I am *never* tearful! And I do try very hard not to give way to self-pity. If ever I am tempted, I quickly look round for something to take my mind off it. Something positive that I can do. Something that will distract me.

I decided that I would pluck up my courage and visit Mrs P. I would do it *right now.* I would find out from her neighbour which hospital she was in, and I would go there that very afternoon. I just hoped it wasn't the same hospital where Nan had been, cos that was a place I didn't ever want to go back to.

I wasn't absolutely certain which flat the neighbour had come from, but while I was dithering in the hallway she suddenly appeared – from Mrs P's! And there was Mrs P, right behind her.

"Oh!" I said. "You're back!" I knew I must have sounded relieved; I just hoped I sounded happy. Cos I *was* happy. "Are you feeling better?"

"She's been badly shaken up," said the neighbour. "I've told her she ought to be in bed, taking it easy."

"Nonsense!" said Mrs P. She sounded almost like her old self, but I could hear that her voice was a bit cracked and crumbly. "I'm perfectly all right! It takes more than some young hoodlum to put me out."

"I was going to come and visit you in hospital," I said.

"Well, now you can come and visit me at home... come in, come in!"

"She ought to be in bed," said the neighbour.

Mrs P waved a hand. "Go away, Betty, and stop fussing over me! Carmen, get inside. What are you dillying about for?"

Me and the neighbour looked at each other and pulled faces.

"In, in! Come along, I don't want to be standing here all day. Have you had any lunch?"

I suddenly realised that I hadn't. I hadn't eaten a thing since breakfast, and I hadn't even noticed! Mrs P told me to go into the kitchen and forage. "You'll find stuff in the fridge. I'll just have a cup of tea."

I thought that really she should eat something, so I did some bread and butter, all daintily cut into triangles and laid out on a plate, and opened a jar of peaches in brandy. I'd never had peaches in brandy, but they looked tempting. At first Mrs P said she didn't want anything, but I was stern with her.

"You've got to eat," I said. "You need to keep your strength up."

"My dear girl," she said, "you sound like someone's mother!" But she ate two triangles of bread and butter and one whole peach, so I felt that I had been right to bully her.

"I'm terribly sorry," I said, "about what happened. It must have been really frightening!"

She dismissed it, airily. "Just one of those things. One of the hazards of modern living."

"I should have gone with you," I said. "They mightn't have done it if there'd been two of us."

"Now, please," said Mrs P, "don't start blaming yourself. It was entirely my own fault – at least, so my friend Betty informs me. Old women of my age ought not to go gallivanting at that time of night. Besides, you didn't want to come with me. I can understand that; opera's not a young person's thing. There's no reason you should be expected to play nursemaid to an old lady. And besides, it wasn't the reason I asked you. You know why I asked you. Don't you?" She looked at me, sharply; obviously expecting some kind of reply. I grunted.

"Did you go away and think about it, as I told you?"

I made another grunting sound.

"Well? Don't sit there snuffling and honking like some kind of animal! What conclusion did you come to?"

I breathed, very deeply. "I s'pose… I'll have to do what you want."

"It's not about what I want! It's about what *you* want. Do you want to be a singer, or don't you?"

"Yes," I said, "I do!"

"Right, well, there you are, then. That's settled. We obviously have a lot of work ahead of us. We should get started as soon as possible! You had better come round tomorrow."

I thought, *Why is she so nice to me when I have been so horrid to her?*

"About midday. Is that all right?"

I said, "Yes!" And then, before I could stop my great clacking mouth I came bursting out with it: "Why are you being so nice to me?"

She raised an eyebrow. "Do you not expect people to be nice to you?"

"Only if I'm nice to them. I've been really rude to you, haven't I?"

"A natural reaction. I'd probably have been rude to some interfering old baggage who kept nagging at me. But the answer to your question is quite simple. It's not that I'm a sweet old lady – well, you've probably noticed that for yourself. It's your voice I'm after! I can't bear the thought of a promising voice going to waste. I should like to think that one of these days I might be known as the teacher of Carmen Bell!"

I smiled, a bit uncertainly. She had to be joking, right?

"My dear," she said, "I'm perfectly serious. You

surely don't imagine I'd waste my time and energy on some rude, sullen girl if she didn't have a voice?"

I grinned at that.

"Smirk as much as you like," she said. "We'll have no more sulks! Now, you'd better be off and leave me to get some rest. I've just been mugged, you know. I ought to be in bed! Don't forget your guitar."

Mrs P came into the hall to let me out. Right at the very last moment I got brave and said, "Did you… actually… see the person that attacked you?"

I wasn't really sure I wanted to know the answer, but I knew I had to ask. Mrs P gave a little snort. (But very ladylike.)

"See? How could I see? They smashed the light bulb!"

"So you wouldn't be able to recognise them?"

"My dear girl, if you had been hit over the head by some young thug late at night I doubt you would be able to recognise them, either. All I was able to tell the police was that it was a black thug rather than a white thug, and I can't really see that is going to be of much help, considering there are countless young thugs of both shades roaming the streets."

I agreed that there were, and that it simply wasn't safe to be out after dark – well, not if you were as old and fragile as Mrs P – but I went on my way feeling a huge surge of relief. I was sorry it had been a black thug cos of Indy being black and people tending to say "Oh, *them* again," which is totally unfair when you think of guys like Lance Stapleton, who has to be just about one of *the* biggest thugs of all time. On the other hand, I couldn't help being glad that it wasn't Lance; I would have hated to feel that I was responsible for what had happened.

When I got home I sent a text message to Josh telling him *OK U win*, and that I would see him on Monday. Since he'd got a black eye defending my honour, it seemed the least I could do. And I owed it to Mrs P. And to Nan. It would have broken her heart to think I'd let myself be bullied into giving up on my ambitions. *Our* ambitions! Nan wanted me to be a star just as much as I did.

I went to bed that night feeling happier and stronger than I had for ages.

CHAPTER TEN

Come Monday morning, I wasn't feeling quite so brave. I desperately didn't want to go and face everybody. Not just Marigold and her mob – all the others, as well. Marigold would be her usual jeering, sneering self, but the others might be feeling sorry for me, and that was even worse.

If it hadn't been for a text message from Josh, and a call from Indy before I was even out of bed – "You are coming back today, aren't you?" – I might have chickened out. But how could I, when they'd shown how much they cared? I couldn't let them down!

This is why you need your friends. You know that they'll support you and stand by you, no matter what. They know that you'd do the same for them.

I don't think I'd have survived without Josh and Indy. Marigold started on at me almost the minute I showed up.

"Well, look who it isn't! Have you come to cross your name off the Top Spot list?"

I wanted so much to say something smart and cutting in return, but I couldn't think of a single solitary thing.

"Marigold reckons you won't be going in for it." Abi Walters, that was. Gloating. "*Will* you?"

Coldly I said, "Why shouldn't I?"

"Oh! No reason. Anyone can enter, I suppose."

"Why don't you just shut up?" said Indy.

"Why don't you, squit face?"

"*Pleeeese*, guys! Don't let's get personal," said Marigold. "She obviously thinks she's going to be another Beth Ditto."

There was a bit of a silence. I concentrated very hard on unpacking my bag. Then a voice said, "Who's Beth Ditto?"

"She's this big gross singer… weighs *fifteen stone*. Plus she's a lesbian." Marigold smiled, sweetly. I felt like hitting her. "Guess that's who you're modelling yourself on?"

I said, "I don't model myself on anybody."

"Really?" said Marigold. "You could have fooled me!"

At that point the door opened and Josh came in. Guess what? Marigold clammed right up. It was like she'd suddenly been struck dumb. She slunk away to her desk and started busily rummaging about inside it, with her head stuck under the lid. She didn't say another word. But at the end of class, as I was packing stuff back into my bag, Ashlee came up to me and said, "I've seen Beth Ditto... She's cool!"

Ashlee, of all people. One of Marigold's best mates!

Indy squeezed my arm and whispered, "See?"

I didn't ask her what she meant; I knew what she meant. I'd plucked up the courage to come back, and that one remark of Ashlee's had made it all worthwhile. I didn't give a toss any more for Marigold Johnson!

Rather to my surprise, I settled in again at school like I'd never been away. I'd only really missed three days, but what with half term it felt like a lot more. If there was anyone thought I'd bunked off cos of all the stuff with Marigold, they didn't dare to say so. I'm sure lots of them did think it, but it was like Josh had become my minder and they were all scared of making any remarks which might get back to him. Which was fine by me! I liked having a minder.

One or two people actually came up to me and said they were glad I was still going in for the contest. They

said things like, "You don't want to let *her* put you off." (Meaning Marigold.) A girl called Julianna that I'd hardly ever spoken to before said, "You ought to have a go! Why shouldn't you?"

Ashlee said, "Yes, why shouldn't she? It takes all sorts."

I wasn't quite sure whether she was being sarcastic or supportive. One minute she seemed to be on my side, the next she was back being Marigold's doormat. It was hard to tell. Anyway, I didn't really care any more. Josh and Indy were there, and they were my friends, and that was all that mattered.

Every now and again I went to see Mrs P, just for an hour. This meant I had to tell Mum. I didn't tell her that I'd bunked off school – I wasn't about to commit hara-kiri, or whatever it is they call it when people plunge swords into themselves. I just said vaguely that I'd "been singing" and Mrs P had heard me.

"And now she's coaching me, Mum! She used to be an *opera* singer. She used to be famous! She's got all these pictures of herself, all dressed up, and all these programmes with her name in. She said I had a good voice and she'd like to be my teacher and—"

"Hang about, hang about!" said Mum. "How much is all this going to cost?"

I said proudly that it wasn't going to cost anything. "She's doing it cos she thinks that one day I'll be a big star and she'll be known as my teacher. If she lives that long. I hope she does! But she's very old. Older than Nan."

"And you say she's *coaching* you?"

"Yes! She's teaching me all about scales and breathing and voice production."

"But what is she coaching you *for*?" said Mum.

"For the talent contest!"

Mum looked confused. "What talent contest?"

"At school. On Charity Fun Day! We're having a talent contest and I'm going to sing this song that I've wrote with Josh."

"Written," said Mum.

"Whatever! It's called *Star Crazy Me* and—"

"You're going in for a *talent* contest? With Josh?"

"No. Just me. Josh is too shy!"

"Certainly not something which could ever be said about you," agreed Mum. "You've always been a show-off! Even as a toddler. Your nan used to encourage you something rotten. God, it used to embarrass me!"

I said, "Why? Cos I was bad?"

"No, because your nan was shameless! She even used to get you standing up in front of total strangers. Even waiting at the check-out in Tesco… *Come on, give us a bit of a song!* Some of the looks we got, I can't tell you."

I didn't remember that. I could see that it must have been embarrassing; I felt quite embarrassed myself.

"Well, anyway, never mind now," said Mum. "What's more to the point, how many tickets can you get?"

I said, "You want *tickets*?"

"Well, of course I do," said Mum. "What do you

think? I'd like a couple, if you can... one for me, one for Maureen. I'm always telling her about you. My daughter with the big voice... She likes your kind of music."

I couldn't believe it! Maureen is the owner of the beauty salon where Mum works. I never thought Mum talked about me at *all.*

"Mind, it's a pity about Josh," she said. "It would have been nice to have the two of you."

I wondered if she was only saying it because Josh looked good and I didn't. I told her again that he was too shy. It's true! He is bold in all kinds of ways, like defending me against Marigold and standing up to Lance Stapleton. There aren't many boys I know would do that. Lance is not only a vicious thug, he is *hulking*. I wouldn't want to get on the wrong side of him! But I can stand up on stage in front of an audience, no problem. I am a bit of a show-off, I suppose. Josh is quite a modest sort of person. The idea of appearing on stage just totally makes him squirm.

After what Mum said, I did have another go at him.

I said, "*Pleeeeze*, Josh! *Pleeeeze* do it with me!" But he wouldn't budge.

He said, "You're the performer. What d'you need me for? All those lessons you're having… you're practically a professional!"

"But we're a team," I said. "It's our song I'm singing! How can I sing it without you?" And then I pulled a really mean stunt. "I s'pose what it is," I said, "you're ashamed of being seen with me."

He told me later that I was lucky we were still talking.

"For that," he said, "I am *certainly* not getting up on stage. But I'll lay down a track for you, if you like."

"Oh, Josh, *would* you?" I flew at him and hugged him. "That is such a brilliant idea! Why didn't we think of it before?"

"We didn't think of it," said Josh. "*I* thought of it. And I might've thought of it sooner if you hadn't gone flouncing about like some great prima donna, having hysterics all over the place."

I said, "Huh! Well, anyway, I'll tell everyone we wrote the song together. You can't stop me doing that!"

"Wouldn't want to," said Josh.

"Couldn't even if you did, cos I shall be on stage and I can say whatever I like!"

Josh said, "Honestly, you can be so childish at times," but I knew that he had really and truly forgiven me and that everything was all right between us.

A week before the contest we learned how the voting was going to be organised. There was going to be a *popular* vote from the audience, with a separate vote from a specially invited panel of experts. The experts were: a man from one of the big music stores in the shopping centre, a man from local radio, and...

TOPAZE! Omigod, I couldn't believe it, I was just so excited. My all-time favourite female singer! And just about *the* most famous person ever to have gone to our school. Well, the only famous person to have gone to our school unless you count a boy called Gary

Mason that grew up to be some big-time criminal that was all over the TV news just a few years ago. Mostly people didn't talk about him. But they talked about Topaze!

Indy was just as thrilled as I was. She is not quite such a big rock fan as me, but Topaze is like a sort of role model for her.

"Imagine! You'll actually *meet* her," she said. "You'll talk to her!"

"Dunno 'bout that," I said. "Person that wins might get to."

"You'll win," said Indy.

But I shook my head. I couldn't imagine anyone as beautiful as Topaze ever voting for a big wobbly jelly like me. She'd more likely agree with Marigold that I shouldn't have entered the contest in the first place.

"Carm, you gotta have *confidence*," said Indy.

I did have confidence – in my voice! Just not in my body. Indy urged me to "Think of Beth Ditto." I didn't know Indy had ever even heard of Beth Ditto, but she said she'd seen pictures of her in a magazine.

"She looks *great*! Cos she's not ashamed, you know? She doesn't care, she just gets out there and does her thing, and everybody loves her. Everybody's gonna love you, too. Just get out there and do your thing!"

Mum, of course, was interested in what I was going to wear. "Put it on," she said. "Let me see!"

I reminded her that I had already shown her. "I showed you when I first got it."

"So show me again!"

Rather nervously, I presented myself to her. Mum is just *so* critical when it comes to clothes. She herself has a really good dress sense, and she is one of those people who always says what she thinks, no matter how rude it might be. If she reckoned I looked like a sack of potatoes, she wouldn't hesitate to say so.

"My God, it makes you look like a sack of potatoes!"

I could just hear her. I braced myself. I said, "Well? Is it OK?"

"It's perfect," said Mum. "Very stylish! But it would be, if it was Josh who chose it. That boy has excellent taste!"

I relaxed a bit when she said that. If Mum approved, it had to be all right. "I'll tell you what," she said. "Tomorrow afternoon, we'll give you a makeover. Face, nails… the full works. Don't you worry! You're going to be a knockout."

I glowed when Mum said that. She almost never praises me, so when she does it is doubly precious. By the time she'd finished giving me my makeover next day I hardly recognised myself! Actually, strictly speaking, that is not true. Mum is a professional. She doesn't believe in turning people into what she calls "caricatures" of themselves – just bringing out the best in them. She didn't use much make-up on me as she said my skin was too young to need it and I already had good strong colouring. (I glowed again!) But she styled my hair, so it wasn't all wild and messy, and she put gorgeous green eye shadow on my eyes, and painted my nails with the purple varnish, and lent me one of her lipsticks, "Deep Ruby", to use before I went on stage.

"There!" she said. "See what a difference it makes? Now you look like a real rock star!"

Looking like one made me feel like one. The Top Spot contest was due to start at six thirty, so Mum drove me to school in plenty of time.

"The last thing you need is to be in a rush. I don't want you getting all hot and bothered and ruining my hard work!"

I was feeling so secure it didn't even rattle me when I heard that Marigold had taken a poll of Year 7 and "Eighty per cent of people said they're going to vote for her sister!" It was Ashlee who told me, all bright-eyed and challenging. Like, *What have you got to say to that?* I didn't have anything to say to it. I thought it was stupid. This was a talent contest, not a general election.

How could you know who you were going to vote for until you'd heard them sing?

A girl from Year 8 advised me to take no notice. "They just told Marigold what they thought would make her happy."

I decided that she was right, and that I would simply forget about it. I had more important things to think about than Marigold and her stupid poll!

When the notice about Top Spot had originally gone up on the board loads of people had put their names down, but over the weeks the numbers had dwindled as people got cold feet and pulled out. Now there were only thirty acts competing. We were strictly limited to three minutes each, including introduction and applause. The rules had been explained to us.

"If you take the full three minutes, we'll have to cut the applause. It's up to you."

Well, I'd timed myself really carefully, with the help of Mrs P. I'd worked out that I could introduce myself, and say how I'd written the song with Josh, in just a matter of seconds, which gave me a good two and a half minutes for the song, and almost half a minute for applause – if anyone felt like clapping that long! Mrs P had warned me that "Half a minute may not *sound* very much, but you try clapping for that length of time and you'll find it goes on for ever!"

We were told that the running order had been chosen by pulling names out of a hat. I was number twenty-eight, which I thought was good. It's always better to be near the end than at the beginning. On the other hand, Mary-Louise Johnson, *damn and blast*, was number thirty. Someone said rather jealously that it had obviously been fixed, but I didn't really see why they would do that. I thought more probably she was just one of those people that was naturally lucky.

We all gathered in the wings so that we could watch what everyone else was doing. Some of the acts were really pathetic. A boy from Year 12 sang an Elton John number and had everyone falling about. The thing is, it wasn't meant to be funny. But his voice kept cracking up and he couldn't stay in tune! Then a Year 11 girl tried to be Madonna. Oh, please! How could she? It was so embarrassing.

Several people, as a matter of fact, came on pretending to be someone else. We had a Christina Aguilera lookalike followed by Katie Melua. Both of them totally *rubbish*. Christina Aguilera had a voice like a bluebottle trapped in a marmalade jar, *bzzzz bzzzz bzzzz*. The other one sounded like a demented car alarm. No competition there!

But then a Britney Spears came on, and my heart sank because she not only looked like Britney she actually sounded like her. She got a *really* big round.

The girl who came after her wasn't too bad, either. Like a miniature version of Jamelia, though I don't think she was actually trying to be. She just *was*. I reckoned she was a possible winner.

After Jamelia there was a boy band from Year 9 that I felt a bit sorry for. They were really cute and they tried really hard, but they were just so bad! Some

people actually started sniggering. I thought that was unkind and I was glad when the audience broke into a huge round of applause.

But then there was an all-girls group calling themselves the Sugar Cubes from Year 10, and I had to admit that they were quite good. The audience obviously loved them; at the end I even heard wolf whistles and stamping feet. Mary-Louise sniffed and said, "Groupies!" but I thought that I wouldn't mind having groupies. Mum and Mrs P were out there, and Josh and Indy, and Indy's mum and Josh's mum and dad, and I knew they would all vote for me, but I couldn't see them stamping their feet or whistling.

When it came to my turn I thought that maybe I would get stage fright again, like I had before, when I sang to the old people. I remembered how my throat had closed up, and how I'd gone all cold and shivery. But it didn't happen! I could hardly wait to get out there and start singing. I did my introduction, then switched on Josh's tape – and that was it. I was away!

Star crazy me
Floatin' free-ee-ee
Into the ether of
Eternity…

Oh, I loved every second of it! I think I must be a natural born performer. I could have gone on and on. I was almost tempted to! But one boy had already run over his three minutes, which everybody agreed was totally bad manners and *extremely* unprofessional, so I contented myself with just repeating the first verse. I couldn't resist! It still gave plenty of time for applause. As I came off, Christina Aguilera whispered, "Way to go!" She seemed to be encouraging me, so I immediately felt mean for thinking that her voice sounded like a bluebottle, even if it did.

The next act after me was a boy who played the drums (not very well) and a girl who screeched. She did! She screeched. It was horrible, like a fingernail scraping on a blackboard. Mary-Louise said, "Forget it!"

And then she was out there herself, all shimmering and shining in a sort of silver catsuit which would have been utterly grotesque on anyone else. She, *unfortunately*, has a figure to die for, and is gorgeous with it. She doesn't have much in the way of a voice, but I thought probably that didn't matter; she was so beautiful she could get away with anything. Besides, not everyone cares about voices the way I do. They are almost the first thing I notice about a person. I know that it's the same for Mrs P, which I think is why we get on so well, in spite of her being ancient and not really caring for my sort of music.

The applause for Mary-Louise went on for ever. Katie Melua said, "Well! That's it, then. We all know who's going to win."

One of the Sugar Cubes said it was like a foregone conclusion. "She was always going to win... people like her always do. They don't have any *talent*, but what's talent got to do with it?"

I thought that was quite brave of her. It was what I'd been thinking myself, but I wouldn't ever have dared say so in case anyone accused me of sour grapes. We all agreed, glumly, that Mary-Louise would win just because she was Mary-Louise and had a following. The only question was, who was going to come second?

After we'd all sung we had a short break while the audience got to register their votes and the votes got to be counted. The boy who had done the Elton John number said, "If I don't come second I'll demand a re-count!" At least he had a sense of humour. I don't think the rest of us did!

At the end of the break we all filed back on stage and sat down on chairs arranged in a semicircle. The three experts sat to one side, while Mr Monckton, who is head of music, took the microphone and prepared to announce the winners. I couldn't help sneaking glances at Topaze. I thought that if Mary-Louise was pretty, Topaze was just, like, *stunning*. Tall, and slim, and golden brown and beautiful. It was hard to believe she had once been a pupil at our dead ordinary school.

Mr Monckton said, "Right! The moment we've all been waiting for… two third places, one from the panel of experts, who chose… Martina Olivera!"

The Jamelia girl.

"And from the audience… The Sugar Cubes!"

Big round of applause. Jamelia and the Sugar Cubes bounded forward to receive their awards. It was the man from the local record store who presented them.

"And in second place, from the panel of experts…"

This was the moment when my throat really did close up.

"The Sugar Cubes!"

Again.

"And the choice of our audience…"

Please, I thought. *Please.* I was starting to feel sick.

"Emily Hadcock!"

Britney Spears. I knew they'd choose her. I watched, dismally, but hiding my true feelings, as the Sugar Cubes bounded forward for the second time, followed by Emily. Now it was the man from the local radio who presented the awards. Topaze was obviously being kept for the winners.

"And finally, in the Top Spot..."

In the Top Spot, in the Top Spot... it was one of those moments when time stood still. I could feel my whole body pulsating, my heart thudding and pounding, tidal waves roaring in my ears. *I can't bear it*, I thought, *I can't bear it! I can't ever go through this again!*

"In the Top Spot we have just the one winner. Our panel and the audience are in agreement!"

My heart sank. That was it. Finish. I hadn't come anywhere! I hadn't even come third. A cold layer of sweat broke out all over me. I had to swallow, very hard, to stop from being sick. Out of the corner of my eye I could see Mary-Louise. Heads were already turning in her direction. She was practically half out of her seat.

"The winner of the Top Spot contest, by unanimous vote..."

There she went! Couldn't even wait for the announcement.

"...is *Carmen Bell!*"

What??? I couldn't believe it. I just couldn't believe it! I stood rooted to the spot, unable to move. Someone said, "Carmen, it's you!" and gave me a shove, which brought me to my senses and made me go catapulting forward so fast I tripped over my own feet and went sprawling. It was Topaze who helped me up. Topaze! My idol! The audience just went completely wild. They were laughing, but clapping at the same time. They seemed really happy for me.

I can honestly say it was **THE MOST WONDERFUL MOMENT OF MY LIFE**. I still couldn't quite get my head round it. *Me*. They'd voted for *me*! I don't think Mary-Louise could quite get her head round it, either, cos she was shooting really filthy looks in my direction. Not at all professional! Everyone knows you have to smile and make like you're happy, even if your heart is breaking. I would have smiled; I was all prepared for it. Pride wouldn't have let me do anything else. As it is, I could feel myself beaming from ear to ear.

Topaze said, "Congratulations!" Her voice was cool and husky, just like when she sings. "You're obviously going to go places. I'm sure we'll meet on the circuit one of these days!"

I tried to say something – like maybe a thank you would have been nice – but all I could do was stupidly grin. And the audience were still going wild!

Everyone on stage crowded round to congratulate me, except for Mary-Louise. They all seemed genuinely pleased that I'd won. Maybe they thought that if they couldn't win themselves then they'd rather it was me than anyone else. They kept saying things like "Well done!" and "You deserved it!" Then I had to have my photo taken – with Topaze and the prize I'd been presented with! – and I just felt so glad that Mum had given me a makeover. I said anxiously to the reporter, "You will say that I wrote the song with Josh, won't you?" and he promised that he would and made a note of Josh's name on his pad.

Afterwards, when it was all over, we went out for a special celebration: me and Mum and Mrs P, Indy and her mum, Josh and his mum and dad. It turned out that Josh's mum and dad had heard of Mrs P. They were quite in awe of her! She must have been a *really* big name in her day. They promised they would give her a lift back home, and I was glad about that cos I just hated the thought of her being mugged again.

Indy said, "Well, come on, let's have a look at what they gave you!"

"It's just a chunk of glass," I said. But of course it wasn't *just* a chunk of glass. It was a chunk of glass with a tiny golden disc embedded in it, and round the side the words ***Winner of the Ravenspark Top Spot Contest.***

"Why haven't you got two?" said Indy. "You came top twice!"

I said that they were probably going to recycle the other prize and use it for something else, next year. "I don't s'pose they expected the same person to win both sections."

"I did," said Mrs P. "I most certainly did!" And then she leaned across the table and took my hand and said, "Congratulations, my dear! You've made an old woman very happy."

That was one of the *best* moments. I knew that next time I went for a lesson she'd be back at her niggling and nagging, asking me if I'd done my exercises, telling me to "Use that diaphragm!", but I would always remember that I had *made her happy*.

Josh's dad had ordered champagne. He held up his glass and said, "A toast! To Carmen."

"And to Josh," I said. "He helped me write the song!"

"Well, then, to both of you."

Everyone solemnly raised their glasses and I felt a bit embarrassed, as I've never been toasted before. Josh looked even more embarrassed! I think he would have liked to hide under the table. But it was OK, good old Indy went and choked herself on champagne bubbles. She complained that "They come down your nose!" What with all the coughing and the spluttering, people stopped concentrating on me and Josh and started thumping Indy on the back and stuffing napkins at her. It was quite a relief!

At the end of the evening, Mum called a cab. Practically unheard of! But Mum said it was such a special occasion it would be a shame to ruin it by catching a bus. To be honest, I'm not sure Mum would know *how* to catch a bus, but she certainly couldn't drive cos of all the champagne, which had made her a bit giggly, so we rode home in fine style.

In the cab Mum stopped giggling and became serious. "Your nan would have been so proud of you," she said. "And I'm proud of you, too! Whoever would have thought it? I'm going to be the mother of Carmen Bell!"

That set *me* giggling. "Mum," I said, "you already are!"

"I suppose I am," she said, "aren't I? I always have been… I just never realised what a talented daughter I had." And then she hugged me, which is something she almost never does. "It seems I've got a lot of catching up to do… I'm going to start boasting about it straight away!"